Tsipi Keller

ITNA

ITNA PRESS
Los Angeles, CA
www.itnapress.com

Cover photo courtesy of f8archive
Cover & interior artwork by ITNA

Bruno's Conversion by Tsipi Keller. — 1st ed.
ISBN: 978-0-9976432-9-9
Library of Congress Control Number: 2023931666

"All was chaos, that is earth, air, water, and fire were
mixed together; and out of that bulk a mass formed—just
as cheese is made out of milk—and worms appeared in it,
and these were the angels."
   —Carlo Ginzburg

"Every sleep is a dress rehearsal
for the great sleep."
   —Irit Katzir

"For years I wandered
  In the world
Now I'm going home
  To wander there."
   —Itzik Manger

He left the hotel at 2:50 p.m., got change at the liquor store across Collins Avenue, and arrived at the bus stop just in time for the three o'clock bus to Aventura. Several people were waiting in line, and he positioned himself politely at what seemed like the end of it. As was always the case when he traveled, Bruno made sure to assume a visitor's benign demeanor, deferential to and respectful of the locals. Here, in Miami Beach, he found himself surrounded mostly by Cubans and was more deferential than usual, as if to let them know that even though he was white, in his Jewish heart he was a minority sympathizer.

His Jewish heart. Only a few minutes before, he'd been lying on his bed, fully clothed, trying to decide what to do with his time now that Mary, whose idea it was to come here, had gone back to New York. As he felt himself drifting off to sleep, the thought came to him that were he to die here in this anonymous hotel room, the only thing he would regret would be having disappointed Rose, his mother. It was a calm observation, curiously painless and neutral, no doubt because he knew it to be fanciful.

There was no need to glamorize his situation. He was stranded, he was left behind, but he was not lost. Indeed, as he liked to tell his students, the real drama often took place not in the visual and tangible, but in the murky domain of one's idle thoughts. Sometimes they came on angel wings, sometimes not.

And then his brain lit up. *Aventura*! He jumped off the bed, grabbed his jacket, and was out the door.

Now, oddly stimulated and pleased he had managed a decision and its execution in a ten minute span, he tapped the shoulder of the man next to him before allowing himself adequate time to reconsider. The man turned, offering Bruno a broad, openmouthed smile.

Bruno hesitated. The man, still young, was missing his front teeth, which gave him a somewhat mad and roguish look. But it was too late to turn away. He had to address the man. "The bus to Aventura?"

The man, still smiling, said, "Soon, soon, just wait here."

Poor, and probably Cuban, Bruno guessed. "How long is the ride?" he asked, if only to mask his discomfort, which, he sensed, the man had noticed.

"Oh, it's long, maybe an hour," said the man, chopping the air above his head as if charting the road ahead.

Bruno nodded, suppressing an urge to rub his palms together as a show of friendliness and goodwill. It was absurd, but all at once he wished for contact, for some confirmation that he existed, that he could still communicate with a fellow human being. He wanted to say more, but found no words to safely express what he felt. The moment passed, and the man turned from him and said something to his companion who responded with what seemed like a lewd gesture, and the two of them laughed.

Somewhat annoyed, thinking he was the target of the joke, Bruno moved a few steps away, busily fishing in his jacket pockets for his sunglasses to protect against the bright but cold Floridian sun. He welcomed a brief spark of renewed hope. Maybe Aventura, as its name suggested, would turn out to be the right place for him on a day like today. As if to spite him, Mary, his shiksa, her face creased with bitterness, made a quick and uninvited appearance, at which time his self-defense mechanism kicked in with the admonition he'd been drilling into his head throughout the morning: *For better or for worse, she left. No acrimony. No self-pity.*

Yes!—He nearly shook with the need to nod his head and re-confirm his succinct formulation. Earlier in the day, before he had arrived at this mature decision, his mind went spinning in the other direction. *I've done nothing wrong. Who does she think she is? And why should I put up with her whims?* Eventually, though, he regained his cool, for what was man if not the putative master of his brain? True, he was now agitated again, but he would calm himself just as soon as he found his sunglasses in one of his pockets. Unless he had left them at the hotel, which would mean he would have to go back and fetch them and miss the bus to the wonder-town of Aventura, if it existed.

Here, he found them. Thank God for small miracles!

He put on the sunglasses, instantly feeling sheltered and aloof. Good. He had decided not to think about her. He had decided to stop settling accounts with her in his head. Now all he had to do was to pull himself together and move on. With time, Mary would be a name relegated to his past, a past populated by others he rarely thought about, people who came to mind fleetingly at distracted moments when he found himself looking back, wondering what had become of so-and-so. Not that he was shutting Mary out. No. He was a forgive-and-forget guy, and were she to make even the slightest gesture, his heart would instantly open to her.

Across the street, a skinny black cat with a white patch between her eyes rubbed her forehead against the pedal of a parked bicycle, and Bruno, charmed, watched her. She seemed peaceful and content, and he wished for the same peace and contentment. A simple life, he thought. Devoid of worldly ambitions. Ambition ate at one's heart and gave nothing back, or, whatever it gave was short-lived. Yes, he had to get himself away from all that was petty and superfluous in his life.

He recalled his father's tales where cats, especially black ones, often represented demons, and throughout his youth, he'd felt a strong aversion to cats, spitting against the evil eye when a black cat crossed his path. Over the years, though, in the homes of friends, he'd learned not to fear them, but rather reach a hesitant hand to their wet nostrils. Now, standing at the bus stop, he wondered if the other cats shunned or feared the cat because she was black. He wondered if, were he in New York, he would take the cat home with him, give her love and shelter.

Yes, he probably would. And she would be a good companion, adding a new dimension to him. He would become softer, more patient, more accepting.

Maybe, he thought further, when the bus comes, I won't get on it. I'll just stand here and watch the cat. Aventura can wait.

He became aware of an uneasy feeling engulfing him, a feeling of desolation, and a powerful urge to be somewhere else, away from everyone he knew, existing in a kind of Eden where he could live simply, absorbing the tranquility of trees and animals, his heart and mind quiet and content.

A bus was approaching, and a few people—mostly elderly women laden with plastic bags—rose from the nearby bench, and soon everyone, including those who had stood in line, clustered in a dense group, waiting for the bus doors to open. Bruno, still unsure if he would get on, let them push ahead of him. Besides, he was in no hurry, and the bus was practically empty anyhow. In this godforsaken place, only the poor used public transportation. All the others sped by in their shiny Lexuses or BMWs.

Finally, he did get on the bus, happy to find a window seat that would afford him an ocean view. The longer the ride, he thought, the better. After all, he was a tourist. The day had been too chilly for swimming, and the early morning walk on the boardwalk— which usually absorbed his thoughts and even got him to hum a random tune—had given him little pleasure. He didn't see the striking, one-legged woman he saw every morning, but the Hasid women were there, some young, some old, sometimes alone, sometimes in groups of two or three. Quite a few of them pushed strollers with the fierce, preoccupied determination of new moth- ers. Some of the younger women carried small weights in their hands, which surprised him. He hadn't known Hasids to be fitness conscious. More so than the occasional Hasid he saw on the streets of Manhattan, these Miami Beach Hasids, especially the women, looked as though they had been airlifted from a Polish shtetl, and their loud, rapid Yiddish annoyed him, sounding harsh in his ears.

Today's *Ostjuden*, he thought. He liked Yiddish, it brought back memories, he liked the idea that Yiddish was kept alive, but he considered it strange and alienating that they chose to speak Yiddish rather than English. He tried not to stare at them, at their long, shapeless skirts, their long-sleeved shirts, their thick, dark stockings, their colorful, yet painfully tight, headscarves. Some of the women had no head covering, and those, he knew, were presumably still unmarried, and therefore not required to cover their hair.

It was a pity they covered themselves from head to toe. Many of them would have been quite attractive if they relinquished their costumes and joined the modern world. In their ungainly outfits, they seemed out of place among the semi-nude joggers, even if the sudden appearance of these exotic turbans and headscarves did make him think of tropical flowers, very much in tune with the dark green bushes and the old and massive palm trees along the boardwalk. When he'd first arrived here a little over a week ago, he had looked askance at them, but as the days passed, he found himself offering an open face, hoping to exchange a friendly smile, which he managed once with a young mother who had bent over the stroller, cooing to her infant and, as he approached, she looked up, giving him a quick, nervous smile, matching the one he had given her.

Interesting that he had to come all the way to Florida to see Hasids on a daily basis. Even the men, not famous for physical activity, took advantage of the boardwalk, and earlier this morning Bruno watched one of them with particular interest: an old, stooped man, possibly a Holocaust survivor, supporting himself with a cane. Large, black earphones covered his ears, and Bruno wondered what kind of music the man was listening to, until it occurred to him it was probably a rabbi's sermon, decoding the Torah or the Talmud.

When the old man left the boardwalk through one of the side lanes, Bruno leaned against the fence and looked at the ocean. Yes, he too was a Jew, but an uncertain, conflicted one, and he looked upon his orthodox brethren with distant, if curious, eyes. He couldn't fathom their belief and how they stuck to it in face of all the ridicule and difficulties. And yet, a part of him couldn't help but admire, perhaps envy, their faith and their apparent equanimity. Was he so much better off than they? They followed the edicts of their faith, he followed nothing, or, if he followed anything, he followed the ghosts of reason, namely, doubts. Personal freedom was sacred to him and his New York colleagues and friends, but freedom from what? And what was he doing on a boardwalk in Miami Beach, watching a group of wet-suited surfers and thinking these circular thoughts?

Well, it calmed him to watch the young surfers, black and sleek in the knee-deep water as they waited for a shimmer of a wave in the calm, turquoise ocean. The horizon, too, calmed him. Linking sea and sky, it was smooth and clear, except for the three military-looking ships Bruno noticed nearly every morning, concluding they must be Coast Guard ships on the lookout for smugglers. It was a well-known secret that Miami Beach prospered thanks to money laundering and drug trafficking, so said Thomas, the guide on the Everglades tour Bruno had taken the day before—the tour, as it turned out, that freed him from Mary, or vice versa.

Yes, the tour that freed him. Them. Thomas, amusing and easygoing, was better company than Mary, if only for the duration of the tour.

"You wouldn't believe the assortment of characters in this area," Thomas had said. Thomas himself was a character, and Bruno took a liking to him in spite of Thomas's beer belly and his thinning, dirty blond hair.

"I'm a transplant many times over," he told Bruno during a coffee break on the way to the Everglades. "I've lived in Brazil, I've lived in Germany, I was a sailor for twenty-two years, and I finally ended up here in Miami, driving tourists around. I guess you can say I've come back to reclaim my American roots, but don't ask me why."

And Bruno, as he listened and watched Thomas smoke and gulp down his beer *(was he allowed to drink on the job?)*, imagined a younger, handsome Thomas, free and wild, tasting and experiencing life in a way that he never gave himself the chance to experience, buried as he was in books and seminar papers. Thomas, for sure, never had to deal with women like Mary. His relationships with women were probably more direct, more physical, and less complicated. When Thomas was done speaking, Bruno sighed and said he would have loved to be a sailor. Thomas gave him a skeptical look but said nothing.

Bruno contemplated the ocean and the surfers, waiting for a wave so he could see them in action and admire their skill. Four Hasid women appeared on the beach and, after dropping their bags and taking off their shoes, they went in, their skirts floating around them as they frolicked in the water, laughing and splashing. He watched them, sharing their childlike delight, until they tired and stood on the beach, while he tried to imagine the sensation of the cold and wet stockings against their skin, not to mention the sand sticking to everything. Briefly, he saw himself married to one of them, and then his stomach made a sound and he consulted his watch; it was time for breakfast.

He turned and walked back, wondering if Mary would still be at the hotel or had already left for the airport, and dreading both eventualities. She never joined him on his morning walks, preferring instead to linger in bed and have breakfast with him when he returned. Not this morning, though. This morning, she would be boarding a plane, going home and leaving him behind, and all because of the Everglades tour. A tour he had taken just to spite her. A tour that had turned out to have been a disaster, even if he'd gotten a kick out of Thomas who had raged against the government and Big Business throughout the trip, while regaling the group in the van with the usual jokes and anecdotes.

And now here he was again, a tourist on a bus, a New York City refugee, a quite respectable, if obscure, professor of French Literature, heading north toward Aventura.

An obscure professor, indeed! It amused him to think he had finally reached the maturity or whatever it took to admit and grudgingly accept it. Yes, as a youth he had envisioned a rich and eventful future, a career of important achievements, but as the years went by, he had to conclude he lacked the nerve and the drive. He had had his moments, yes, in front of a class or when he was on a stage receiving an award or being recognized and honored by this or that institution. But such moments came and went, leaving nothing in their wake. Deep inside, he still harbored a dream, humbler and narrower in scope, wishing for a quiet life with a partner, writing a book about his father.

A tiny, nearly invisible bug kept flitting near his nose, and Bruno waved his hand to shoo it away, at first calmly, and then with mounting irritation. He looked different from the others on the bus, and he worried that those around him questioned his sanity as he fought the tiny, perhaps imaginary bug.

Finally, the bug left him, and he was free to study the faces of the youngsters who got on the bus along the way and stood in the aisle, boys and girls on their way home from their last day at school before Christmas break. He observed them with mild curiosity, entertaining the thought that he could have had a son, that he could have had a daughter. He looked out the window, hoping to catch a glimpse of the ocean in between the tall hotels and condos that rose to the sky in jarring angles.

Relentless verticality—the phrase rang in his head. He had come across it recently in a book or a magazine but couldn't remember the context.

He became aware that a woman a couple of seats across was staring at him. He did his best to ignore her, but every so often, compelled to see if she was still watching him, he shifted in his seat or scratched his head while sneaking a glance in her direction. She had short brown hair and bulging brown eyes, and her bottom lip protruded in a permanent pout. Like him, she was white, no longer young, and possibly a tourist as well; a large bag sat on her lap, her hands clasped tight around it. Her expression, he thought, was hostile and tense, but for all he knew, his own expression seemed hostile and tense to others. It was a war of attrition—age and the stress of years did this to your face. Your eyes lost their youthful, open gaze. They seemed tired when you were not tired; they reflected disillusionment even when you didn't feel disillusioned. The face he saw in the mirror and often looked at with affection was not the face others saw.

He straightened up in his seat and released the top button of his shirt. There. Much better. Self-awareness yes, self-recrimination no! A war of attrition or not, he was still alive, still part of human society, even if with each passing day he felt more and more unsure about things. But the faces of the schoolkids around him looked fresh and smile-ready, inviting his sympathy. Carefree, their voices rang out melodiously, their sentences usually beginning with *pero*, with the occasional *claro* thrown in. He knew some Spanish. He liked the sound of *pero* and *claro*, and this set him to mull over why the Yiddish bothered him while the Spanish pleased him, admitting to himself that the overt Jewishness of others embarrassed him, as if he and the Hasids were related through guilt and shame.

Shame of what? Tribalism? The shadow of pogroms and the Holocaust? Every time he heard a reference to Hollywood and *The New York Times* "elites," he heard "Jew" and shrank a little. In this cowering attitude, perhaps he, the emancipated, freethinking liberal, was the classic Jew, more so than the Hasids, more so than the Jews who did open their mouths. The Jews who protested the plans to build a convent in Auschwitz. The Jews who monitored the media for anti-Semitic/anti-Israel bias. Mary, his wonderful *shiksa*, liked this about him, appreciated that he wasn't a "Jew." But was she aware that in his heart of hearts he thought of her, at times with tenderness, at times with animosity, as his *shiksa*? It was ironic, he once told Mary, that Jesus's famous injunction to turn the other cheek, had come, over the centuries, to epitomize the Jew's *de facto* status of a meek and passive subject, persecuted as he was by the two giant siblings Judaism had spawned. "Call the pope," Mary retorted offhandedly, and he had to laugh.

The bus crossed a long, concrete bridge, and, for the whole stretch, he could see the water without obstruction. A few white sailboats perched along the horizon. Such calm and serenity, he thought, longing to be out there on the water, maybe on one of those sailboats, with friends, with a lover, a glass of white wine in his hand. There were pleasures to be had; one only had to reach for them.

Bruno sneaked a cautious glance at the woman with the bag. Alas, she had given up on him and was now leafing through a magazine.

On the floor of the bus, an empty plastic bottle rolled and stopped under his seat, and Bruno, annoyed, kicked it backward hard and tried not to think of the *shiksa,* now probably back in her Midtown apartment, while he was on his way to Aventura, not because he had heard it was an exciting place to visit, but because it was easy to reach, and it got him out of the hotel with a resolute step and a plan in his head. He and Mary had come this way a few days ago when they drove from Miami Beach to Ft. Lauderdale to explore the area. They had planned to stop in Aventura on their way back to the hotel and didn't, but promised themselves to go see it another day because the name intrigued them. When they first landed in Miami, they had rented a car, and then gave it up. The drivers here, Mary complained, were reckless; she and Bruno were safer paying for a cab to get around or taking advantage of the cheap and convenient public transportation. This way, she said, we can see what the natives are like.

He had to agree, not least because Mary was in charge of the driving. He still kept his license in his wallet but had lost the habit, having sworn off driving years ago after a crash that nearly killed him. They had come here with the idea of spending their first Christmas and New Year's together in snowless Florida, while looking into buying or renting a two-bedroom condo for periodic escapes from New York. But Mary quickly changed her mind about living here once it became evident they would need a car.

"This is the true face of America," Mary grumbled. "Cars and anonymity. We're hooked on speed. No wonder we're so irritable. I can't imagine living here. At least in New York I can see people's faces. I can jaywalk!"

"I agree," he said, and, for a moment, they looked at each other, content in their shared New Yorkness. Still, he felt he could live here during semester breaks, with or without Mary. He thought he would treasure the quiet, the isolation. He would find a favorite outdoor café for breakfast, preferably facing the sun, a place for lunch and dinner, and a bar where he would sip his after-dinner liqueur and engage in conversation with an occasional stranger. That was all he would need: establish a routine that would ground him in his new, temporary home. The boardwalk, he felt sure, would rescue him every morning and set his mind straight, and he would soon adapt to life without Mary, even if his stubborn brain kept going back to the last image of her from early in the morning when he rose quietly and stood a moment looking at her sleeping on her side before he left for his morning walk. And perhaps not so much the image of her as the nagging thought that it had all been his fault, a thought he hoped to banish with the manic repetition: *No acrimony. No self-pity.*

There was sudden movement on the bus, and Bruno came back to the here and now—it was the last stop. Aventura Mall, the driver announced, and Bruno got off, a bit uncertain now that he had reached his destination. The woman with the large bag stood on the pavement, and then hurried toward another bus, taking her farther north, Bruno supposed. He walked away from the bus station, heading east, trying to get beyond the tall buildings and find his way to the beach.

Aventura, he soon realized, was all concrete, massive and gray, with residential towers and huge parking lots, and roads and overpasses going every which bewildering way. There were no people on the streets, only speeding cars, and he felt as though he had entered a de Chirico painting. He tried to keep his spirits up, but he retreated deeper and deeper into himself, and, as if a child again, walking hand in hand with his mom, he murmured the letters of street signs and license plates. He crossed roads and walked through one parking lot to another, getting nowhere. A FedEx van was pulling from the curb, and Bruno waved his arms and ran over to the driver's window to ask the way to the ocean.

The man, youngish, with red hair and red eyelashes, observed him through pale rheumy eyes. He took his time answering this very simple question, and Bruno wondered if perhaps he seemed wild, maybe even demented. It was windy—he could feel each individual hair at the top of his head pulling at the roots.

"Are you driving?" the man finally asked.

"No, walking."

"You can't walk there, it's too far."

"How far?"

"You can't walk there. You need to take the highway, and you can't walk on the highway."

Bruno watched the FedEx van drive away. So much for Aventura, he thought with self-derision. The stranded, desperate tourist, looking to find something to do while far away from where he belongs—home.

Mary the Absconder was home now, moving about in her apartment, comfy among her meticulously selected and neatly preserved tchotchkes, looking over her mail or chatting on the phone, telling friends she was back and open to invitations. She had chosen to flee and leave him behind on a whim for no good reason at all. Well, let her live with her choice. The two of them usually had good fun in and out of bed, so how could she just give up on him and leave?

It wouldn't surprise him if, right this minute, she was dramatizing the breakup scene for Joyce, her best friend, and this, in fact, did bother him quite a bit because Joyce, whom he kind of liked, would naturally side with Mary, while he would never be given the chance to tell his side of the story. Joyce had dubbed her ex-husband an "angry radical feminist" because he insisted women should carry their own weight. He never opened a door for her, and wouldn't dream of helping her carry her luggage when they traveled.

And what if he and Mary got back together? How could he look Joyce in the eye? Or how could Joyce look him in the eye? Well, who said life was neat and tidy?

At any rate, for the time being, he had nothing to complain about. So far, the few hours with Mary gone had been quite all right, peaceful in fact. He didn't have to think about her, to plan his day with her, to get her permission to do this or that, to worry about pleasing her, or, God forbid, disagreeing with her. The tyranny!

He turned and walked back to the mall. The sight of an old woman behind the wheel of her car cheered him somewhat. She was a tough-looking blonde with a focused gaze and a cigarette stuck in the corner of her mouth, and he said to her in his head, *more power to you, lady.* She could have been his mother, but Rose dyed her hair black and lived in Baton Rouge.

By the time he reached the mall, he regained his calm, willing to reconsider, to forgive and forget. Mary left because he upset her. No harm done, just a short hiatus apart. In a few days they would reconnect in New York and try to work it out. Most relationships were trying, especially for people who lived in the city. Everyone was harried and not always at their best, and the fits and starts he and Mary were experiencing were to be expected. In addition, as one grew older, the aptitude to be intimate with someone new took time, possibly because of an overused or abused limbic system, not to mention the many hurdles and disappointments suffered in the past, which caused one to behave in ways that made it difficult to connect. The spiraling, vicious cycle only got stiffer as one aged.

Bruno pulled the heavy entrance door to the mall and walked inside. The gigantic ground floor was devoted to food. People young and old sat at plastic tables and ate from plastic plates. It was one large jumble, and the place hummed with the noise of shoddy living.

"Posterity!" His brain offered a Jules Renard quote. "Why should people be less stupid tomorrow than they are today?"

He didn't consider himself a snob, and yet at times, as if against his will, he felt superior to those around him. If Mary were next to him, strolling through this vast pastiche of fast and cheap, she would find just the right—and cutting—word to describe the place and her reaction to it. And he, as if compelled, would play devil's advocate, saying something like, "These people are the salt of the earth," and she would snap and say that he always contradicted her, and he would deny it, and they would fight and not say another word until he offered an apology.

Why did he contradict her? Because if he wanted to be absolutely honest with himself, he would have to admit that too often he didn't like her. He craved her company, but he didn't like her, and he didn't like himself when with her. She was sharp and intelligent and even mesmerizing—at least in his skewed perception —but he was tense around her. Maybe he had come to Florida to cleanse his heart. Maybe it was God's doing. Maybe it was good she'd packed her things and left, allowing him to take advantage of the respite and, hopefully, rejuvenate himself.

Or maybe not. Maybe he had already begun to miss her. Could he ever be a hundred percent sure of what's in his heart? She was mean to him, and yet he missed her—was he a masochist? Men often were, he mused, when succumbing resignedly to women and their judging ways, if only to keep the peace. Most women, he thought, were mini-tyrants and, more than once during their seven months together, he came to realize Mary had a nasty streak she wouldn't or couldn't control. She was the type who forgave herself, but not others. She never doubted herself or her judgment, and he, like a child, had to rebel.

But she was also a charmer, and even as he contemplated these negative aspects of her personality, he also knew she meant every word she said in the moment she said it. And when she laced her arm through his or put her hand in his and squeezed it, saying: "I do like you sometimes, my sweet Bruno," his heart opened to her, wholly and fully committed.

One of his fondest memories was the morning they sat face-to-face in a café in SoHo. It was their second or third date, and she arrived in yellow flip-flops and a light summer dress, her blond hair pulled back in a ponytail, and, over a cup of coffee, she casually said, "I think it's best if you and I allow ourselves time to see if we like each other as people before we jump into bed," and he, charmed and relieved that she had taken them so far so quickly, said, "Yes, of course," and she continued, "For me, sex is more than just an exchange of fluids," and he smiled and said, "Yes, for me as well," and at that moment, something changed in her eyes, and he saw she had made up her mind to want him.

Yes, she was shrewd and seductive and, in all probability, did manipulate his feelings, good or bad, and he let himself be like putty in her hands. She had a dark spot on her lower lip, and he always found himself watching it while she spoke, recalling Miss

Lukasic, his first grade teacher, with whom he had been madly in love. During class, he would fixate on her lower lip where a drop of spittle would soon appear. He would watch it grow and become thick and white, like a pearl, and he would wait for her to lick it off, and then a new one would begin to form.

He took the escalator up one flight and walked through one store after another. They all looked alike and offered the same merchandise—aisles upon aisles of shirts and pants and more shirts and more pants, all crowding together on racks and hangers. Who would ever buy all these *schmattes*? he wondered. Was there a graveyard for *schmattes* nobody wanted? Rose had told him she now thought twice before buying a garment or even a kitchen utensil, asking herself if she really needed it. When he visited her a few months ago, she showed him her closets.

"See?" she said, her voice vibrating with pride. "I cleared out my closets. I gave away everything I don't need or use anymore, just in case I die tomorrow or am diagnosed with Alzheimer's, like Molly." Molly, her sister. "I don't want you and Alexie to be burdened with having to sort through the stale debris of a lifetime."

"But what about memories? Things you're attached to?" he asked, looking at the neat, nearly empty shelves.

Rose let out a chuckle. Living with his father, she said, she had learned that getting attached to possessions was a bad idea.

"But you're not Father," he said, and Rose said, "Yes, I am, and you are, too."

Of course, he knew as much, and when he said she was not Father, it was his mouth speaking. His mouth, and his desire to comfort her, to take her mind off death and Alzheimer's, but she was too clever, a cold realist thinking ahead.

"Everybody around me is on antidepressants, it's depressing!" Rose chuckled. "I tried to organize an exercise class in our building. I even gave it a name: Get in Shape Not in Pain. I hung posters in the lobby and in the elevators, but no one was interested. And I was offering it for free. Go figure. They're perfectly content to sit all day on their patios and discuss their doctors and the number of meds they swallow every day. Sometimes I want to scream at them. They take a nap after a meal, and when they wake, they plan the next meal. They complain that their body is not what it used to be, that they feel old. Well, hello! Get off your butt and do something. Jump in the pool, take a walk, for crying out loud, do something! "

"Maybe they're tired," Bruno suggested. "Maybe they're kind of tired of living? I mean, what do I know?"

"Well." Rose lingered, and Bruno worried he had said the wrong thing. He hoped she would counter and say something like: Well, they should fight it every minute of the day, like I do, but she simply said, "Well, yes, I guess."

"Remember the *siddur* Father gave me when I turned thirteen?"

Rose looked up at him. "Of course I remember. Do you still have it?"

"I'm sure I do, I just have to look for it. It's probably in a desk drawer or on a bookshelf."

"I couldn't tell you then, but I can tell you now. Father and I used to laugh between us at how passionate you became, reading in that book. You took it all very seriously. You even tried to lecture Alexie, which didn't turn out so well."

"No." Bruno smiled, recalling his obdurate, overbearing sister. "It didn't. I'm a failed rabbi."

One more floor and I'm out of here, he decided, and took the escalator again, climbing the steps as they bore him upward. Here, it was more *schmattes* and accessories, sunglasses and umbrellas, hats, and gaudy custom jewelry. He touched a leather belt, thinking maybe he should buy it, but was unable to muster the necessary focus to engage in commerce. In spite of his aimless wandering, he didn't feel gloomy or depressed. He was where he was because he had taken a trip and come here to explore whatever there was to explore.

In a way, the vacuity of the mall fused nicely with the vacuity in his head. Normally, he would never walk into a store without a definite purpose in mind, but today as a vacationer and tourist, he was allowed to go blank and waste time. Time, in fact, was of no consequence. It sort of dissolved, abolishing itself. He didn't have to think of work. His computer and phone had been wisely left behind in New York, so he was unreachable, free to do as he wished, just amble along with his ruminations, his reliable companions.

Waiting for the bus to take him back to Miami Beach, he stationed himself next to a smallish, elderly lady, who licked her ice cream with a greedy tongue. Chocolate chip and vanilla, he guessed. He licked his lips and swallowed the saliva gathering in his mouth. He should have gotten some ice cream. Strawberry and peach, maybe, and pistachio, too. He watched the little old lady, remembering that the greed of old people made him uneasy, it seemed vulgar somehow, but he soon reminded himself in a few years he would be just as "old." She, too, was a blonde—most of the old ladies in Florida were blondes, he noted—and a tiny shopping bag was looped around her arm. Unlike him, she had found something to buy.

"Useless calories," she suddenly said, looking up at him. "I don't do this very often, but I felt like it. Sometimes you just have to obey your body."

Bruno smiled and nodded. "Absolutely," he agreed.

The two of them stood a bit away from the bus stop sign, catching a last ray of sun. It was five o'clock, and the bus, he hoped, would arrive momentarily. A cold wind was still blowing, but standing in the sun warmed him a bit.

"Do you live around here?" he asked in a gentle voice.

"I used to come here with my husband," the woman replied.

"Ah," Bruno said. "You don't live here, then?"

"Only in the winter. I used to come here with my husband," she repeated, maybe inviting him to inquire about the husband, but at this moment his mind was set on practicalities.

"Did you buy a place here?"

"No, I'm renting," she said between licks. "I live in New Jersey."

"Hmm," he said. "How much do you pay, if I may ask? I'm looking to rent a place myself."

She turned away from him, and, for a moment, he worried he had been too forward. "Here comes our bus," she said, beginning to walk toward the bus stop, and he, the dutiful son, followed behind. "Eighteen hundred," she said to him over her shoulder. "It's a nice condo. I always rent in the same building."

She took the front seat, right behind the driver. Hesitating a moment, thinking she might invite him to sit down next to her, he then nodded in her direction and continued farther into the bus, taking a seat by the window. Now the Intracoastal, rather than the ocean, was on his right. The sun, he noted, had cracked open, spilling gold and orange across the sky. It seemed painful, like a birthing, and just as bloody—there was something gory about its splendor, and it took his breath away. Along the road, trees came alive with the chatter of birds. He couldn't see them, but he assumed they were the black birds he saw everywhere: on the boardwalk, on the beach, and at the edge of the pool at the hotel, where they dipped their long beaks and satisfied their thirst, not minding the chlorine. There were also mourning doves everywhere, clean and elegant in their brown-beige coloring and the white collar around the neck.

The orange-gold light spread farther and lower in the sky, losing definition and turning pink. Where clouds had been only moments before, remnants of gray were hanging below the pink, layering the firmament and giving it the form and texture of huge, prehistoric wings. He became aware that he was composing a description in his mind, a composition he would later offer to Mary, but since Mary was no longer an option, then to someone he might meet while having dinner or a drink at the bar. A man or a woman, it didn't matter.

He looked at the sky, modulating his thoughts, recalling Tolstoy's admonition that if you looked at something with the aim to describe it, you ended up not seeing it at all. But he was seeing it with watchful, admiring eyes, wishing to share it with someone, even with a stranger who might think him lonely and a bit dotty.

An old man was giving the black female driver an argument— she had neglected to tell him where to get off. The woman from New Jersey was conversing with another old blond lady. They could have been sisters. Sitting side by side, they looked alike in their hairdos and profiles. Observing it all, Bruno began to feel alive, even hopeful. I feel mellow, he told himself, melting and spreading like the dying sun. He thought about what he might have for dinner, maybe Italian, maybe Cuban—something garlicky and spicy, something that would please his nostrils and his taste buds.

The driver stopped the bus and let the old man get off, even though it wasn't a regular stop. Good riddance, someone said, and the people up front laughed to show their solidarity with the driver. Of course, if one of them were to miss their stop, they wouldn't be laughing so hard. People were cruel and thoughtless in petty ways, like the Dutch couple he had met during the Everglades tour.

They were tall, in their sixties, and quite athletic and healthy-looking. In the van, they sat across the aisle from him, and at first he thought they were German. But, as they inundated Thomas with questions and compared American dairy products ("lousy") with Holland's milk and cheeses ("fabulous"), he realized they were Dutch. He didn't speak to them, but he noticed how, when the group got off the van for a break, the wife would extend her hand like a beggar, and the man would reach under his windbreaker, unzip a pocket hidden under a flap, and produce his fat wallet.

They seemed well-suited to one another. A kind of understanding or conspiracy seemed to float between them, and if at first he was indifferent to them, as they were to him, their apparent self-centered complacency soon began to grate on him, and, as the day progressed and the ritual around the zippered hidden pocket was repeated, Bruno's annoyance turned to silent, seething resentment, and by the tour's end he actively loathed the man, including the wife in her supporting role. They were driving back from the Everglades, it was getting dark, and Bruno watched as the man, in the dimness of the van, unzipped his pocket once more, fished out his wallet, and carefully brought out two dollar bills---a tip for Thomas. It took all of Bruno's self-control not to point out to the man that a two-dollar tip wasn't adequate. It wasn't so much out of concern for Thomas's finances as much as the insult such a puny amount implied. To get the couple's attention, Bruno, very deliberately, coughed and took out his wallet, pulled out a twenty and held it in his hand, hoping they would get the hint that here he was, a single person, tipping twenty dollars, and that they, a couple, should tip at least as much. Bruno knew that the husband had noticed the bill in his hand, but his efforts were in vain, for the husband did not reach into the sacred pocket again.

Back at the hotel over dinner, he told Mary about the zipper and the fat wallet, and she twisted her lips and said it was none of his business what people did with their money, and how much they chose to tip or not to tip a guide. He said that was not the point, and she said, "What is the point?" and that was the beginning of the fight that finally made her board a plane and leave him behind. "You're too judgmental," she continued, proceeding to quote Machiavelli, something to the effect that people are wondrously blind to their own shortcomings, but are quite the implacable prosecutors when it comes to the faults and vices of others. "But that perfectly describes you"—Bruno, out of breath, nearly shouted in the restaurant, a no-no with Mary, who turned white and said, "Enough already."

Up in the room, he tried to apologize—for what?? He agreed with her, he said. Indeed, it was amazing how people viewed other people's affairs in black and white while allowing themselves every kind of shady leeway and rationalization. It was comic, really, and yes, he, too, was not faultless, but, he hoped, to a lesser degree. After all was said and done, she had to agree that he was open-minded and tolerant on most issues. He wasn't such a terrible person, was he?

She heard him out, contemplating him with large pensive eyes, and he thought he was gaining her back, but then she said, "We're not right for each other, Bruno, don't you see that?" And he, physically and emotionally drained by then, said that yes, he did see it, even though he didn't, not really, and then the thought hit him that, had Mary joined him on the tour, he wouldn't have noticed the zipper and the wallet. "You should have come with me on the tour. Then we wouldn't be having this silly argument. We would have been together, like a normal couple, like the Dutch couple," he tried to joke.

Mary, as if appreciating his efforts, gave him a feeble smile. "Something else would have come up, eventually," she said, pulling her suitcase out of the closet.

"What are you doing?" he asked, feeling silly, like a character in a B movie.

"Packing."

"We have another week here."

"Not me. You can stay if you like, I've had enough."

"But, Mary," he said, reaching for her, but she waved his hand away.

"My mind is made up," she said, thus sealing the argument and chilling his heart.

That night, they slept in the same bed but far and apart from one another, the wide, king-size bed accommodating their rancor.

Needless to say, he hardly slept, while she, probably with the help of one of her melatonin pills, slept soundly. He tossed and turned on his side of the bed, nightmarishly rehashing the events that had led to his present misery. What upset him most was the realization that had he given up on the idea of the Everglades tour and spent the day with Mary by the pool, none of this would have happened. She didn't want to go, she was not fond of swamps and mosquitoes, and even though the concierge had assured her there would be no mosquitoes this time of year, she refused to go. She had come here to rest, she said, preferring to stay by the pool and read a book.

At this point, as he sat there, half listening to her and the concierge, gazing at the small sign on the desk: **It's nice to be important, BUT, it's important to be nice,** his desire to take the tour began to wane. But then Mary, as was her way, added with a haughty laugh that a trip to the Everglades would be too much like a program on PBS, a gratuitous remark that injured the concierge—Bruno saw it clearly on the concierge's face—and on the spot he booked the tour, which, it turned out, had been a mistake. He didn't enjoy himself, and in the deafening noise of the airboat, instead of looking for alligators like all the others, he found himself studying the earlobes of the man seated on the bench directly before him. They flapped in the strong wind, and Bruno, anxious, touched his own earlobes to ascertain with relief they did not flap. The earlobes of the man's wife also fluttered, and her hair, in the blowing wind, had parted in the middle, revealing the silver and gray layers underneath the blond. People were vulnerable when they least suspected it, Bruno reflected with a touch of desolation.

When morning finally came, careful not to wake her, he slipped out of bed, got dressed, and then stood a moment watching her. She slept on her side, with both palms under her right cheek. She seemed troubled, as if condensed into herself. He tried to evoke feelings of tenderness toward her, but his heart or whatever it was that usually stirred in him when he watched Mary sleep, was now stilled. He turned and left the room, heading to the boardwalk as he did every morning. Maybe he should have stayed and talked to her. Maybe she would have relented, but he was tired of begging, tired of playing the penitent role she had assigned him.

Mary, his *shiksa*. He had his own set of grievances, but what was the point of voicing them? And maybe it was true what they said. Maybe it was wiser to stick to one's own kind. He didn't really believe it, but sometimes the thought did nag at him that Mary could never deeply and truly understand where he came from, just as he could never understand where she came from. Indeed, some time ago, as he and Mary sat down to dinner, he casually remarked about the fact that the church used bells and that the mosque used a *muezzin* to call the faithful to prayer, whereas the Jews had no use for bells and whistles. They went to prayer or did not, and Mary said, with a vehemence that surprised him: "That's because your religion is primitive."

But then, he and Ellen, his Jewish ex-wife, also quarreled, and so did his sister Alexie and her husband, Gerry, with Alexie winning all the fights as Gerry, a quiet, mild man, gave in to her. Alexie was a year older than Bruno and always reminded him she came first. She ran her own ad agency, smoked two packs a day, and lost her temper at the drop of a single syllable. He often wondered how her employees could stand her.

"The louder you scream, the louder you tell the world that you're wrong. When you're angry, you become stupid, your I.Q. drops. And that's a fact!" he once told her, and she threw a vase at him. She was an optimizer whose life, at all times had to be in absolute order, and any momentary glitch or deviation from the scheme she had devised for herself and others drove her mad.

More absurdly, she wouldn't rest until she was convinced she had found the best of whatever she was looking for. If she was in the supermarket buying three lemons for a dollar, she had to be sure she was getting the best three lemons available for that dollar.

So, the fact that he and Mary fought had nothing to do with religion. The only woman with whom he was able to find real peace and solace was Rose. He would be embarrassed to divulge this to a shrink, as well as the realization that, while he yearned for a Rose in his relationships with women, he always, somehow, ended up with an Alexie. Or a Mary.

And yet, he reasoned, it wasn't necessarily the male/female thing. People's egos clashed. Their pride was a shield, but also the cause of the myriad ways they felt hurt, slighted, stepped over. There were moments of grace, but the fundamental state was one of conflict, of thwarted efforts, of heartache and remorse. If he and Ellen had had a child, perhaps things would have turned out differently. But Ellen, whose job required frequent and long travels, wasn't ready to have a child, and he, busy building his own career, did not insist.

There was no message for him at the hotel, but he called Mary anyway, worrying he would get her answering machine and would have to leave an awkward message, a message she would listen to and then erase. He didn't want to call her, and even as he picked up the receiver, he told himself not to call, he didn't feel like talking right now, but he did, punching her number slowly as he rehearsed what he would say to her, not so much the phrasing as the attitude and the tone of voice he would assume, a natural and affectionate tone, which should indicate to her he was above the petty calculations of who did what and who was to blame, and that he was prepared to forgive and forget and give the two of them another chance.

No. He'd rather leave a message than talk to her. Her voice might trigger a Mary-antibody he wouldn't be able to rein in. But she picked up on the second ring, her "hello" crisp and cool and familiar. She had forgotten all about me already, he thought, then cleared his throat and said, "Hi, there," sounding phony and ro-bot-like.

"Well, hi there to you, too."

"How are you?"

"Fine. How are you?"

"I'm okay. How was the flight?"

"Good."

"It's strange." He tried to cackle amiably. "Strange that you are in New York and I am here in Miami Beach."

"Maybe."

"It was your idea to come here," he reminded her, his Mary-antibody starting to agitate.

"So?"

"Nothing, I'm just… well, it doesn't matter."

They waited. He imagined her sitting on the couch, her feet, gloved in white wool socks, resting on top of the magazines on the coffee table, looking at one of the blown-up photographs she was proud of. Possibly the one on the wall above the TV, depicting the World Trade Center in flames, juxtaposed with a colorful Lego tower, a photograph he couldn't even look at, thinking it sophomoric and in poor taste. He wished he could get up and pace a little, but the telephone cord was short, forcing him to stay hunched over at the edge of the bed.

"So," he said. "You landed all right?"

"Obviously."

"Miss me?"

"Not yet."

"What are you doing?" He thought he sounded friendly, casual, and even managed to put a smile on his face, regretting she was not in the room to see it.

"Doing?"

"Yeah, like, I don't know, making dinner or something?"

"Or something, yes."

He breathed. "You're not very forthcoming."

"Forthcoming about what?"

She was toying with him, but he answered levelly, with a hint of mirth in his voice, for indeed, the ongoing farce began to amuse him. "This conversation?"

"That's the way I am, Bruno, don't start," she said, then added after a millisecond, "please."

He muffled a sigh, searching his brain. "Frankly, I don't know what else to say. My thoughts are a bit confused at the moment. I've had a strange day. I mean, maybe not strange, but not very uplifting."

"What did you do?"

"I took the bus to Aventura. The ride was okay, but Aventura itself... I felt as though I had entered a prison."

"Hmm," she said.

"Not very cheerful, am I?"

"That's all right," she said in a soft, almost comforting voice. "You're going through a phase."

"I am?" He was relieved and grateful to hear her say that, not because he thought it was true, but because it meant she had been thinking about him, about the two of them. Maybe it was true, maybe he needed guidance.

"I think so, Bruno. I've only known you a few short months, so who am I to say, but you've changed. You were more fun when I first met you."

"Well, it's always more fun in the beginning, but I see your point," he said, humbled. "The thing is, the entire world, it seems to me, is going through a phase, and we're all affected by it. The thing is, I want to talk to you, but I don't know how. I want to talk to you about real things and not about Aventura, for instance." As he was speaking, it hit him that they had never said the words, "I love you," to one another. "You know," he continued, "it occurs to me now that I never told you that I loved you."

"Do you?"

"I don't know," he admitted. "And you?"

"I don't know either."

He felt a pinch in his chest. It hurt him to hear that, but then, he had just hurt her with the same admission.

"Well, may I call you when I come back to New York?"

"When are you coming back?"

"In a week, as we had planned."

"Sure," she said, after a pause. "You can call me."

"I thought you might, well, not want to have anything to do with me. I annoy you too much."

"You're not annoying one hundred percent of the time. You have your good points. You redeem yourself sometimes."

Well, it was good to hear he wasn't annoying one hundred percent of the time.

"By the way, it's snowing here."

"Just in time for the holiday," he said. "Merry Christmas."

"Merry Christmas to you, too." And, as the debate went on in his head whether or not to say, 'We were supposed to spend it together, our first Christmas and New Year's,' she said, "I know what you're thinking."

"So, I won't say it." He smiled. "Are you going to Joyce's?"

"Probably. I'm sorry you'll be spending it alone, Bruno. I mean it."

"I know. I guess I'll survive it somehow."

He waited for her to hang up, then he put down the receiver. He poured himself a generous portion of whisky and walked out on the balcony to take in the evening air and calm his nerves. He shouldn't have called, but modern life made instant communication so easy. People automatically reached for the phone when it was better to remain quiet. The unwelcome result was a queasy feeling in his core, and possibly in Mary's as well. He should have waited till tomorrow, allowing the two of them time to reconsider and simmer down.

He also had to contend with the fact that the reason he called her was his fear that if he waited till morning, she would think he had been waiting for her to call, and since she hadn't, he'd capitulated and called her.

He also expected a message from her when he got back to the hotel, even just a short, curt one to let him know she had arrived safely.

Truth be told, he did feel a bit disoriented when he entered his hotel room, now empty of her. If she had called and left a message, he would have returned the call right away and then booked a flight to New York.

Bruno looked up at the darkening, deep blue sky. He sipped his whisky, recalling palpable moments of pagan-like worship, especially when he had occasion to share his awe with someone at his side, to point up to the sky and say: "Look how beautiful the sky is." And that person, let's say Mary, would look up and say, "Yes, it is beautiful," and they would stand a moment filled with gratitude for the sky and for themselves, their couplehood.

Now, on the balcony, he tried and failed to retrieve that kind of mental uplift, which got him thinking about what was commonly called the "spirit," the "soul" where such uplifts are stored. And if the gift of worship was stored in him, why couldn't he summon it at will? He had recently read an article that told him he was nothing but a particular arrangement of particles, and that somewhere in infinite space in a parallel universe there existed a planet just like earth, where an exact copy of him lived the exact life he was living, making the same mistakes he was making, and thinking the same thoughts. It was an intriguing and strangely comforting notion. He wanted to believe it, even though he couldn't fathom it.

There were no stars in the sky, so he looked down to the lit pool and the palm trees framing the pool deck. The scene below was hushed and calm, but a tension gathered in his body as if he were waiting for something to happen, as yet unclear if this something would be good or bad. Every morning, a man—a local, Bruno judged from the man's deep tan—did his yoga stretches on a mat, then jumped into the pool. He was bald at the top of his head but still managed to sport a long and blondish ponytail. Every morning after his walk, while waiting for Mary to get ready, Bruno went to the balcony and watched the man, appreciating the meticulous and religious solemnity he devoted to his body. He was probably in his forties, a bit meaty around the middle, but his chest and back were hairless, wide, and smooth, which, Bruno thought, must be appealing to women.

"A fag," Mary remarked one morning when she joined him on the balcony. She was buried in the large white terrycloth robe the hotel provided, a robe she liked because it was soft and made her feel luxurious. Something in her offhand remark about the guy annoyed him. The remark and the spurious luxury of the robe made her look clumsy somehow.

"I don't think so," he said. "He's probably the yoga instructor at the health club."

"Right," she said, turning to go back into the room.

"Why are you so——?" he called after her, not finding the right word. "And even if he is gay, so what?"

"So nothing," she said and went in.

Wishing to avoid her, he remained on the balcony and continued to observe the man, who, his routine done, jumped to his
feet, folded his mat, and went into the pool, where he stood on
one leg and stretched the other against the ledge.

Then Ellen quietly and shrewdly slid into his mind. Ellen doing her evening yoga routine on the living room carpet, following
the instructions of her yoga tape, while he sat in his armchair and
read a book, or graded students' papers. Even toward the end,
when their marriage was a series of fights and complaints and he
had lost all desire for her, when she lay on the floor, with her long
legs up in the air, something stirred in him and he wanted, however briefly, to love her all over again, tempted to rise from his
chair and touch her and maybe rekindle all they had lost. They
had been very much in love at the beginning, he now recalled with
a nostalgic pang.

They were a new couple, setting up a household and a future,
and Ellen, when not shopping for kitchen utensils and skimming
recipes in magazines, was on the lookout for healthy, sprawling
ferns she hung from the ceiling, usually near and over windows.
He would have preferred an open, clear view, and as much light
as was possible. True, the view from their windows wasn't very
inviting—rooftops and a narrow strip of sky—still, he preferred
it to the nuisance of hanging plants.

But, as is usual in such matters, Ellen was in charge of the
décor, and he yielded to her. Besides, she was emotionally attached to the plants—some of them had come with her from her
studio apartment—and he couldn't *deprive* her. She talked to them

in soft tones, played classical music she thought they liked, and often caressed them. When away on business, she would call and ask, "How are my babies? Did you remember to water them?" and he had to admire her dedication.

And so, he endured the plants, but every so often when bending to open or shut a window, he banged his head against the base of a clay pot and quietly fumed against Ellen and the plants. Once, when she was away and he was in charge of watering the plants, he climbed the small stepladder, lost his balance and crashed to the floor, pulling the plant down with him. Sitting on the floor amidst the wreckage, he cursed and vented, and then, soothingly talking to himself, he got up and cleaned up the mess.

He replaced the plant, and when Ellen returned from her trip, he noted, with relief and glee, that she hadn't noticed a child had been switched on her.

How fickle the heart, or what we call the heart. Ellen ended up claiming he didn't have a heart, but he did have a heart. He felt it beating in his chest, *fortissimo*.

While he was watching the yoga man and reminiscing about Ellen, Mary reappeared on the balcony, this time wearing the pale blue cotton dress with the spaghetti straps she knew he liked. She had a nervous constitution—or was it metabolism?—that kept her slender and a touch too bony, and with her sharp little nose and newly cut short blond hair she looked boyish, youthful.

She put on the dress to please me, he thought. He wanted to put his arms around her and hold her, but her voice stopped him.

"I'm hungry, Bruno, are you ready?"

"Yes, but first…" He took her into his arms. She was stiff with resistance, her hands pushing against his chest, but she smelled good, and he drove his nose deeper into her hair, still damp from the shower. He sniffed at the roots, determining from the faint sour odor that she had rinsed her hair but not shampooed it. She shampooed only twice a week, and on non-shampoo days, dabbed some cologne on her hair, but it didn't help much. In fact, it fused unpleasantly with the odor of the scalp. He often considered telling her this, yet could never bring himself to do so, knowing it would embarrass her. Maybe now was the time, he thought, and then in a flash, a dream-image from the night before came to him, and he remembered how he had sunk his hands in the soft white fur of a goat, and how pleasant it felt.

"Let's go," Mary whined, "I'm hungry."

"Maybe I could eat you, and you could eat me," he said, rubbing his nose against her forehead, and Mary pushed him away.

"I don't like you this morning," she said, "but I'll let you buy me breakfast." She released herself from his arms and looked down. "He's still there, your Apollo."

"He's not my Apollo, but he could be yours."

"Not my type, he's too physical."

"So he's not a fag."

She regarded him a moment. "I don't care if he is or isn't, why are you so hung up about it?"

"I'm not hung up about it, I just don't understand why you said—"

"Sometimes, my dear, you're just too literal-minded. Let's go."

—what was the use? And why the prevalent vacillation in body and mind?

He gulped down the rest of the whisky and walked back inside, leaving Mary and Ellen in the chilly air of the balcony. He took a shower, shaved, and dressed with care as if for a date. Tonight, it would be just he and himself for dinner. *Tant pis* or maybe *tant mieux*. He walked along Collins Avenue, then turned right onto Lincoln Road, where restaurants lined the sidewalk and many of the shops were open late into the night. He studied the menu boards of a few restaurants, finally deciding on the Italian restaurant where he and Mary had eaten a couple of nights before. Even though the night was cool, he took a table on the sidewalk, the only diner choosing to eat outside. When he had been here with Mary, they'd sat inside, both of them noting with a New York City approval that the waiters were all Italian, which was a good sign.

The waiter fawned over him, even placing his hand on Bruno's shoulder when leaning over to point out a dish on the menu

Bruno was holding. The waiter's attentions made him feel good, if a bit uncomfortable, he being so much older. The waiter suggested seafood ravioli as an appetizer, then the veal cutlets, and Bruno agreed, asking for extra garlic "on everything."

After he placed his order, he watched the activities next door where a new jewelry store, *Time for Gold*, had its Grand Opening party. Loud salsa music poured from within, and people, mostly blond girls in flimsy black dresses and ridiculously high heels, walked in and out through the open doors, smiling self-consciously and sipping champagne from plastic flutes. Something told him they'd been hired for the night to attract passersby into the store, and yet, he sensed a hesitancy in their manner.

The more he watched them, the more his heart opened to their youthful innocence, prompting a fatherly smile at their naïve belief that they looked glamorous. He recalled Thomas's words: "What more can you expect from a place where Al Pacino's *Scarface* videos and posters are prominently displayed in stores?" This was the land of pirates. Cigarettes and hard liquor were cheap, wine and fruit were expensive.

Maybe Mary had a point: this wasn't the paradise they'd envisioned when booking their trip. Still, he had every right to resent her for shrouding his fantasy in negativity—she had been negative and snippy almost from the start—but now that she was gone, it all looked even more unreal to him, and people on the street seemed more disconnected from one another than they seemed to be in New York. But, he reasoned, it was also possible that the disconnectedness in New York was more familiar to him and, with time, he would adjust to the locals. Wasn't man, after all, the most adaptable animal of all?

Here he was, a man in his fifties, of solid bearing, alone in a place that meant nothing to him, a place he knew nothing about. Maybe he should have done some research before coming to South Florida, but he never planned in advance. He always let others—Mary, in this instance—busy themselves with the details, if only to avoid arguments and disagreements. But even this, what he considered to be his affable, easy-going side, got him in trouble with Mary. He was lazy and selfish, she claimed, never offering to help, always leaving the legwork to others. And so, any way he looked at it, he had only himself to blame. Maybe he was selfish, like Mary said.

"But isn't everybody?" he ventured once, and she rolled her eyes, then cast a scornful glance at him that told him he was hopeless. So, why do you stick with me? he thought of saying, but, of course, didn't. He wasn't selfish, not more so than Mary and his circle of friends.

As a matter of precise fact, having grown up with a father who quoted from the Talmud—instructing his son to never shame another in public—he was considerate of others. He did his best to avoid hurting another, quite often depriving himself of voicing a grievance or delivering a clever but cruel repartee. His father and mother were his models. His father, who told him that if one managed to survive the first few weeks of a Nazi concentration camp, he began to understand the how and the why of tyranny's appeal, inviting him to relinquish responsibility for his fate, which for some became yet another form of survival through abdication, placing their trust in God.

As Bruno was having his ravioli, a young couple arrived and, after a moment of indecision, sat down two tables away from his. Soon, the waiter arrived, and they ordered a bottle of Chianti, accepting his recommendation. Bruno continued to eat, but he was no longer at ease. The couple, he sensed, were looking in his direction, maybe watching his plate.

He finished the ravioli and leaned back in his chair, waiting for the veal and watching the people strolling past, smiling, waving, and talking. They inhabited a different world, he thought, parallel to his. They were real people leading real lives. While they joked and laughed and made merry, he was busy thinking his thoughts, always trying to figure out this or that, often brooding futilely over a thoughtless remark or gesture.

Instant comfort came when Stendhal joined him at the table, Stendhal who envied the good bourgeois who concerned themselves all day with the price of wheat, the health of their horses, their mistresses, and their money. He envied them and coveted their vulgar happiness and their easy contentment. And yet, Bruno thought, it was not wise to lump all bourgeois together. For all his brooding, he too, was bourgeois, and, on the whole, had done well for himself and for those around him. He had a couple of good and reliable friends who, like him, were divorced. His colleagues, though, were all married with children, and when he listened to their domestic problems, he commiserated with them, even dispensed advice, while secretly blessing his good fortune. He missed out on familial joys, but was equally spared the agony and turmoil, the constant and noisy involvement with spouse and kids.

Living alone, there were no emergencies in his life and, most mornings, he remembered to be grateful. Upon waking, he found himself, with a touch of wonder, re-welcoming the fact of his existence with the thought: Here I am, still alive, still able to get up and out of bed. Thankfully, Rose, nearing eighty, was healthy and active, but Bruno's father had died at sixty-two of a heart attack, while he was hitchhiking in Europe. He had learned about the death two weeks later when Alexie finally tracked him down. He cut his trip short and flew back home to be with Rose.

The veal was a bit overcooked, but he didn't want to make a fuss and bother the friendly waiter. After all, this wasn't his last meal. Besides, the ravioli was good, and one out of two wasn't so bad. The couple brought their heads together, laughing into each other's mouth; Bruno gave out a small, audible sigh. They were young and in love, he was allowed the gift to sit side by side with the future, so blissfully clear and rosy, so moist, at this moment at least, as the boy licked the girl's nose. The other night, with Mary asleep at his side, he was surfing the channels when he came upon a scene from an old movie, depicting a young couple lazing about and kissing on a blanket, a late Seventies song blasting from the radio of their red parked car.

Ah, to stretch out on a blanket alongside your sweetheart, kiss and fondle her while a favorite tune played on the radio.

True, he was not a stallion of twenty, but he still had these feelings in him, so maybe he wasn't that old. Only fifty-five but aging. He didn't feel fifty-five, but there it was, a number that meant something, a number he recalled every time he strained himself hauling a piece of furniture or lifting his laundry basket and muttering in spite of himself, "A man my age shouldn't have to do this."

Going down to the laundry room in the basement was a mental ordeal because of the women he encountered there, usually the Hispanic or Polish maids of his neighbors. He felt awkward among them, especially when he stuffed his sheets and towels into the machine, mindful of every move he made, convinced that every eye in the room was set on him. And if he happened to drop an item on the floor, he blushed like a boy. They seemed to pity or reproach him for not having a maid or a wife to do his washing. He saw himself in their eyes, an okay-looking man, but possibly the victim of some defect, which explained why he was without a wife. Of course, he had the means to hire a maid, but he couldn't imagine allowing a stranger free access to the mess in his closets, not to mention the occasional yellow stain on his underwear.

But if Mary was gone from his life for good, would he ever meet someone who would love him? Was he still loveable? Or even likeable? In the coming days and months, if a woman were to look at him as a potential candidate, would she be wondering about his teeth and gums? About his odor? About how he looked with no clothes on? Was it all downhill from here, or did he still have a few good years left in him? How fortunate he felt when he and Mary had first met, fortunate and certain the two of them would end their days together. How naïve he was, or maybe just too eager for love and companionship. Not on bread alone and so forth. Not on sex alone.

Real fears, real concerns, and yet, the mirror in his bedroom told him he still projected the *bonhomie* of a good-looking man, attractive in an old-fashioned, intellectual sort of way, in a Marcello Mastroianni sort of way, or so he had been told: affable and a bit removed. At Mary's insistence, he had joined a gym where he worked out with a trainer twice a week and did thirty laps three times a week, but his stubborn, middle-aged belly still protruded a little.

More importantly, he was aware that his spirit, his soul, had gone soft, maybe numb, and often, when out in company, he was actually bored, but, like the others, he joined in the eating and drinking, laughing at the jokes. His students and colleagues thought him patient and tolerant, but the truth was he had dressed his resignation in forbearance, and every once in a while, upon waking, he felt he had to reignite the flame that kept him going, like one putting a match to a stove's pilot light.

At times, though, when he caught himself running after a bus or zigzagging in the crowded streets of New York late for class, he did marvel, with a touch of humor, at his own stamina, at the fact that he was still in the race, animated like any youngster. And unlike men his age and older who dated young girls who could be their daughters or granddaughters, he himself did not go for girls.

They didn't interest him. He couldn't help but look at them with amused, sympathetic eyes.

But the women he did date, women in their late forties, tended to be cranky and cynical. Mary, for example, and all the others he had met once he and Ellen divorced after a fifteen-year marriage. Fifteen years! It was hard to grasp, but a significant chunk of his life had borne no fruit. What he did learn in subsequent years was that more often than not, middle-aged women grew hard, as if something had shut down in them. But men, too, hardened. He felt it in himself. It was possible that Ellen had been the best, and he had let her slip through his fingers.

Ellen was remarried for the third time and "blissfully happy!" as she made sure to tell him every time they spoke on the telephone. He winced whenever he heard it, not because it hurt him, but because she didn't sound like herself when she said it. And the more she repeated the same "blissfully happy," the less he believed her, even as he wished her all the best. She had moved to Florida with her new husband, a rotund, corporate lawyer, and lived in Tallahassee. He thought he might call her once he and Mary arrived in Miami, but didn't.

He felt beaten down, so he straightened his back and shoulders to chase away the defeat in his bones. Thinking about aging and death gave him masochistic pleasure, possibly because death was a border he would have to cross—schooled, but not prepared. Many times he was on the verge of asking Rose if she thought about death. The subject of death hung in the air between them. He wished to clear it, but couldn't bring himself to actually speak the words. It would be, he feared, an invasion of privacy and, worse, a kind of affront, as if telling his mother, "You're old, you'll be dead soon." It was easier to imagine himself a stooped old man, strapped in a wheelchair in the corridor or the TV room of a nursing home, trying, with the last vestiges of willpower, to keep his head up to observe those around him. He imagined his skin craving someone's touch, perhaps a nurse's or a visitor's. He saw the brown plastic tray before him on the white Formica table as he waited to be fed some runny, beige-gray gruel.

A few more years, he thought. After that, he'd be gone, dead and buried like his father. Or even if he got to live longer than his father, he was still living the last years of his life. He had read somewhere that castrated men lived longer, so this too was an option, a stab at longevity. More and more, even moments of joy felt hollow. Even when he laughed wholeheartedly, he heard the echo of his laugh, keenly conscious of what lay ahead.

Maybe really old, like seventy or eighty, when one was possibly more inclined to accept one's fate, was better than this not-here-not-there stage, when one still had a youthful look. When one could still pretend he was in the thick of things, a man in his prime, all the while sniffing death, all the while aware that a fresh supply of young men joined the marketplace every day, and that he had to step aside to make room for them. They were the innovators. They set the tone. So, maybe seventy-eighty would be better, but Rose had recently told him peace was never a permanent thing, not when you were twenty and not when you were eighty. She had just met a new suitor, whom she liked at first, but after a month or so of dating and, presumably, sex—Bruno didn't dare ask—the new suitor told Rose he wanted to have the freedom to date other women.

"I can't believe it," Bruno had exclaimed. "How old is the man?"

"Eighty-three."

"Eighty-three! And he wants to date other women?"

"Well, why not? He's in good shape."

"Still, who does he think he is? A Casanova with dentures? How many women does he think he can date?"

"As many as a thirty-year-old. Nothing changes when you're eighty, Bruno, not in the mind, anyway. Besides, men have no shame."

Bruno took a moment to think. "Are you upset?"

"Duh," Rose said, giggling like a girl for having used "duh," and the realization hit him that the woman at the other end of the telephone line was very much alive and of the times. The woman he thought of exclusively as his old and aging mother had fantasies and desires that had nothing to do with him or with her being his mother.

"Well, you can date others, too," he offered, an idea that popped into his head as a fitting solution to the problem.

"Sure. Like there's an army of eager octogenarians out there breaking down my door."

Bruno laughed, imagining Rose fighting off an army of octogenarians.

"Frankly, Bruno," Rose continued, "when these old men look at me, they see an old woman, forgetting, or wanting to forget, that they are old, too. That's one benefit of a long marriage. Your spouse looks at you with the same eyes he looked at you when you were twenty. I always looked at your father with the same eyes that saw him for the very first time when he was nineteen and I was seventeen."

"Was he handsome?"

"Oh, yes, he was absolutely gorgeous, like a god." Rose sighed. "But I have to look ahead and take what's coming."

"You miss him." Bruno ventured.

"No, but I think of him often, especially in the morning when I wake up. And, it would have been nice to hear my god snore next to me once in a while." Rose laughed, and Bruno laughed with her.

So no peace, but hope, ever eternal. Even if he got to live to be eighty or ninety, who would mourn him? And what exactly was this tremendous, obstinate will to live? To get up every morning, consume more or less the same meals, go through the same practiced motions. You knew your way in your kitchen, your bathroom, you had the same random thoughts, saw more or less the same people, had more or less the same conversations.

"How was everything?" The waiter appeared at his side.

"Oh, just great, thank you."

"May I offer you our delicious Italian espresso? Dessert?"

"No, thanks. Just the check, please."

"Of course," the waiter said in a less cheerful, perhaps hurt voice, and for a moment Bruno reconsidered, prepared to ask for the dessert menu, but the waiter had already walked away, and Bruno relaxed. The party next door was winding down. The girls had tired of smiling. One of them began to walk toward him like she knew him, but soon realized her mistake and retreated, sending a small, apologetic smile his way. The young couple leaned back in their chairs and puffed on their cigarettes. This was how time trickled away. Sometimes you were aware of it, sometimes not. It was better not to be aware of it, not to think too much.

The will to live. Was it pride, competitive pride? To stand and be counted among your contemporaries? To live at least as long as they did? He recalled a night when he and Mary were having dinner at Joyce's, and how the two women discussed aging and menopause as if he weren't in the room. Joyce talked about how happy she was, having said goodbye to her Tampax. "Good riddance, and not a moment too soon." She laughed. "I gave them to my daughter."

She talked about her vagina losing its grip, and she proceeded to tell Mary about this instrument she had just purchased on the advice of her gynecologist, a kegelmaster, a pelvic exerciser which worked the kegel muscles of her vagina and made them stronger and more effective during sex. She recommended it to Mary, but Mary said she had her own methods, exercising her muscles the natural way. She didn't like the idea of pushing metal implements into her body.

Bruno sat and listened, marveling that they didn't seem to mind him sitting there listening. They more or less ignored him, which he took as a compliment. They trusted him enough to let him share in their confidences. He was a women's man, Mary had said, and he felt special, privileged. Joyce had just come back from a trip to Portugal where she'd had a fling with a local lawyer she had met in a bar and who, after two nights of wild love-making and beautiful romance—or so a trusting Joyce believed—ditched her. He had whispered endearments in her ear for two straight nights, and then made himself scarce, unreachable on his cell phone or his office.

It was Joyce's secret, and yet Mary told him about it, which, Bruno thought, she shouldn't have, and she even included intimate details he would have preferred not to hear about, such as the man telling Joyce that she was as beautiful on the inside ("meaning her sex," Mary emphasized, just in case he didn't get it) as she was on the outside.

Mary had also told him that upon returning to New York, Joyce had enlisted the help of a Brazilian man who worked in the supermarket where she shopped, and together they composed a nasty letter in Portuguese that Joyce faxed to the lover's office.

"How could she do such a thing?" Mary had said to Bruno. "What did she expect? Wedding bells?"

And Bruno said he thought revenge was the right response— humiliate the bastard in his place of business, and he and Mary, of course, fought again.

"Your check, sir." The waiter, bending over, placed a small dish on the table. He lingered. "What a beautiful night," he called, spreading his arms and audibly taking in a breath of air.

"Yes," Bruno agreed, distractedly. "It's snowing in New York."

"Is that where you're from? New York? I love New York. A great metropolis. I love the people."

Bruno took out his wallet. "Can you recommend a friendly bar around here?"

"Friendly." The waiter thought it over. "A bit risqué is okay?" he asked, smiling.

"Why not?" Bruno smiled back, his heart swelling with sudden, vague apprehension. Was the waiter suggesting a prostitute? "What's the name of the place?"

"Snow White. You take the first right up the block, and you'll see it. It's just around the corner, you can't miss it."

Bruno looked up at the waiter. He had a petite goatee that rendered his face longer and narrower and gave him a charming, devilish look.

"It's very becoming." The words flew out of his mouth.

"What is?"

"Your goatee."

The waiter smiled and reflexively stroked his chin. "Don't forget, Snow White," he said and went back inside.

Maybe he could do this, Bruno thought. He didn't want a prostitute, but he could go to the bar like someone who goes into a movie house for the air conditioning. Maybe he would surprise himself and engage a prostitute, if he chanced upon one who didn't look like one. Or he'd be content to exchange a few pleasantries with a man like himself, adrift in Miami Beach.

He tried to smile at this, but emptiness gnawed at him. Yes, he was adrift. He felt lost. It had been so long since he had felt real and profound joy. The sadness and gloom he had been carrying around were not new. They had been festering in him these past few years and were the source of a bitter arrogance, an arrogance that came from feeling excluded from what he saw around him. Even his work no longer offered solace, no longer had the power to save or to heal him.

As far as he could trust his memory, he had begun to feel alienated from the city as it mushroomed and thrilled with the frenzy and excesses of the nineties. Like a new password or a new and accepted addiction, money was on everybody's lips. As the moneyed moved in, the poor were driven out. Young and old, people on the street occupied themselves with a variety of gadgets, plugging their ears and staring at screens, deaf and blind to what's around them, be it a person begging for a quarter or a person asking for directions. Sharing the street with these chaotic and oblivious walking talkies, he had to navigate and get out of the way to avoid colliding with them.

And then 9/11 came. For the first few months afterward, he felt connected again, in love with the city and its people—they all seemed a bit subdued, humbled, perhaps even contrite. Every time his eye caught the digits 9:11 on his watch, he re-experienced the whole of the tragedy in one short instant, followed by a haunting premonition of doom. They had become vulnerable, a society conscious of imminent danger, and this gave them pause, but not for long. Perhaps it was in the city's blood, in its nature, for excess and ruthlessness took hold all over again, more so than before. Inane TV shows and talking heads set the intellectual and emotional tone, and again he felt out of touch, aloof, and disconnected.

Maybe it was time for another terrorist attack, he thought. Maybe we are asking for it. Maybe there is a punishing God. Maybe we are the citizens of Sodom.

He needed to escape. Maybe it wasn't too late to start a new life in a fishing village somewhere. Last March, sometime before he met Mary, he had gone to Mexico, to Akumal, a small village on the Mayan Riviera, and for the first time in years, he felt thoroughly at peace. The relentless New York engine that accelerated his heartbeat and forever drove him onward—if there was such a thing as onward—shut down in Akumal. His brain and heart had gone quiet. No doubts or bad thoughts assailed him.

Gradually, the familiar New York arrogance that had animated him in the city left him, and upon realizing the change, he blessed his good fortune. He took long walks, swam, and learned how to snorkel. He felt no need to watch TV, to read the paper, or to get online. He was perfectly happy offline, technologically absent, but emotionally and spiritually very much present with the fish, the trees, the birds, and the friendly, smiling Mayans. Like them, he rose with the sun, and after dinner by nine or ten, satiated with food and water and sun, he was reading in bed until it was time to turn off the light and give himself over to the hum of the ocean and sleep. He spent only ten days in Akumal, but at certain moments it felt as though he had been there always, as if everything that had come before never really happened, and any lingering memories of another time were in fact the memories of a stranger.

Yes. There was nothing to stop him. He could, if he wanted to, take early retirement and quit the race, effectively make himself disappear.

His brain lit up, and a decision formed in his mind. He would do it. As soon as his time here was up, he would go back to New York, put his affairs in order, and depart. Mary would come and visit if and when she wanted to. He would bring along his computer, his dictionaries, and hopefully work on a new book, a book he had always wanted to write, the story of his father's survival during the Nazi regime.

In the main, he wanted to love every day of his life, every day that was still left him. Love every day of his life and feel that it was meaningful. Only in Akumal—he thought—where he had discovered in himself the language of his soul, would he be able to commune with his true, higher nature and gather the necessary love and focus to write his father's book. If in New York he felt like an alien, in Akumal he felt he was one with life. There was no divide between him and all that lived around him. If in New York he dwelled on death, in Akumal he felt alive.

Better yet, he simply lived from moment to moment.

No, he decided. He would not go to Snow White. He didn't want a nightcap. He did not feel the need for aimless chit-chat. He paid his bill, thanked the waiter again, and walked back the way he came.

Next morning, he opened his eyes at 6:39. It was still dark out, too early to rise, so he lingered, gazing at the sky beyond the balcony. All was calm, and he lazily followed the low-level activity in his head, thinking of rising or not rising while trying to determine if he had had a good night's sleep.

Yes, he did.

Mary beckoned from her corner. He acknowledged her presence, then concentrated on a dream-image that hovered suggestively at the edge of consciousness. Once he got firm hold of the image, the dream would surface, hopefully intact.

The dream-image proved irretrievable, but then, with sudden clarity, he remembered: Akumal! The paradise he had resolved to return to. He would have to plan carefully. Consider all the "for" and "against."

What if the paradise he remembered with such longing no longer met his needs when he went back as a long-term resident?

What if he felt alone with no one to talk to?

No matter how self-sufficient he thought himself to be, he did need people, he did need to feel he was part of a community. Oftentimes, just walking the familiar streets of his neighborhood around Seventieth Street and Columbus, he felt he belonged, sharing the pavements with, and the destiny of, those around him.

Maybe he'd been a bit hasty, making such a sweeping and radical judgment about his life in the city. Even in the worst of Sodoms, a few kindred souls were always to be found. If he truly felt passionate about writing his father's book, he should be able to write it anywhere. If the romantic idea of escape appealed to him, he should, at the same time, leave the option of a return open. He could, of course, sublet his apartment rather than sell it, but then he would be worrying about the stuff left behind: his books, his paintings, his files.

Bruno took a deep breath. He didn't have to figure it all out right this minute. Whenever ready, he would deal with all the issues he would have to deal with. He could put his things in storage. Wherever he went, he could have his mail forwarded. At any rate, he would not teach anymore—about this, at least, he had no doubts. And, if he did leave for Akumal, or another oasis, he would take along his father's Bible and yarmulke.

His father hadn't been religious in the strict sense of the word, but he respected tradition. He trusted the poetic truth of the Old Testament, and Bruno too, during his boyhood, was some kind of believer. He liked the heroic tales about the kings and prophets. He loved the handsome and fearless David who defeated Goliath, and he grieved for Samson who became blind and suffered a tragic, if ultimately glorious, end. He liked the festivities around the holidays, and Friday nights, he went to synagogue with his father, where he sat, feet dangling from the bench, and watched all the Jews around him, wrapped in their *talliths*, davening.

Bruno turned onto his back and shut his eyes, seeing himself for what he was—a man alone, sprawled in his pajamas on a king-size hotel bed. He and Mary had made love on this bed, vowing to make love in every state of the union. Next time they spoke, he would remind her of their vow. They had been tender with one another, exchanging long, unhurried kisses, luxuriating in the velvety sweet taste of tongue and saliva, the same tongues that delivered biting remarks. When their egos were at rest, they were teenagers again, discovering for the first time the tactile pleasures of skin and flesh.

Under the cover, his hand sought the warmth of his groin. He wondered how many others had made love on this bed and how many others had ruined their vacations quarreling in this room. He liked hotels. He liked to unlock the door and walk into a hushed room, curtains drawn against the sun, and find that some magic hand had come and made his bed.

The fresh white towels on the rack, as well as the sheet of the toilet paper folded into a triangle, pleased his eye. Every day, he looked for the small, individual touches the chambermaids had left. Each had her own personal flair, usually evident in the artistic folding of the washcloths, at times in the shape of a flower, sometimes in the shape of a tube, sometimes laid on the rim of the bathtub, sometimes on the bed, with two small hand soaps sticking from their folds. And even though at home he favored open windows and fresh air, in hotels he was willing to cede control to central heating and cooling systems, accepting the fact that windows would shut out the world beyond.

At 7:10, he got himself out of bed, peed, brushed his teeth, and put on some warm clothes. Before putting on his socks, he checked the skin between his right pinky-toe and the toe next to it. A burning sensation had been bothering him off and on for the past few months. When it first began, he thought it was a fungus of some kind, but the skin was clear, and he decided it was God's subtle way to remind him that he was fallible.

Still, aside from minor aches, he was healthy, his annual check-ups and test results were good, his blood pressure was low, and his good cholesterol was high. Quite unusual these days, his doctor had said. Why unusual? he asked. Because we're leading unhealthy, stressful lives, she said flatly, putting aside his chart as a signal that his time was up and another patient was waiting.

He crossed Collins Avenue without having to wait for the light. It was Saturday morning and there was very little traffic. Two elderly drunks sat on the pavement, a bottle of vodka between them, discussing God in earnest.

Everybody got up in the morning, Bruno reflected. The wretched, and the less wretched, each of us waking to our own package of pains and worries. Each of us possessed of a brain. That ever-active, fearful organ, bent on survival.

He reached the boardwalk and, as was his habit, turned left, heading north. The walkers and joggers were already there, and he recognized a few of the faces—regulars, like him. The thought pleased him that he, too, was a regular, at least for the time being. He wondered if they were natives or vacationing tourists.

A woman came toward him, the narrow triangle of her pussy discernible through the thin cotton of her tight, gray shorts. Down on the beach, a small film crew was setting up for a shoot, and he wistfully recalled how he, in his youth, was part of such a crew, filming outdoor scenes in the streets of Manhattan for a low-budget student project. How proud and special they felt, convinced they were doing something terribly important, while trying very hard to appear professionally nonchalant when passersby stopped to watch.

Bruno's nose filled with liquid, and he leaned over the railing and blew it into the bushes. He'd never done such a thing before, and he was surprised by the ease the stuff just flew out of his nose. You've never done such a thing, Bruno, he chided softly, suddenly brimming with positive energy. A Hasid and his two young sons walked past him. They walked fast, probably on their way to *shul* for the Sabbath morning service. The man carried a plastic bag in his hand, and Bruno thought of the string he had learned about at the hotel, a string that stretched the length of the boardwalk to accommodate the Hasids who, according to their laws, were forbidden to carry anything across "zones" on the Sabbath. And so the string, affixed on poles and lampposts by the city, rendered the four-mile boardwalk a one-zone area.

On the grass beyond the fence, an old woman was setting up a picnic for the stray cats of the neighborhood. She pulled dishes and bowls from a large bag and filled them with food and water. There were such people all over the world. Bruno had seen them feeding stray cats and pigeons. Usually old people, usually poor—only they, with their meager resources, found the time and the will—and Bruno marveled at their dedication, at the impulse behind this kind and caring gesture.

And then, his heart skipping a beat, he noticed in the distance the one-legged woman coming toward him, keeping her usual brusque pace on her crutches. The first time he saw her, it had been a hot day. She was wearing white shorts, and it took him a moment to become aware of her deformity. She seemed to be in her late thirties or early forties, the owner of strong, attractive features and a mane of wavy, brown-reddish hair.

Good genes, he thought, wondering how she had lost her leg. Some kind of car accident, in all likelihood. She looked too healthy to have suffered a disease that would have required amputation. Today she was wearing long black pants, and the empty right pant leg blew grotesquely in the wind, calling attention to the missing limb. He felt awkward and embarrassed for her, wishing she had worn a skirt or a long dress.

He was so intent on watching her, his step faltered, but he soon recovered and, as they drew near, he prepared to say hello, to smile, but her severe expression, possibly due to the strain of hoisting herself forward, discouraged him, and they went past each other with the blank faces of the strangers they were. Maybe tomorrow, he thought, as he asked himself what he could possibly want from her. He would be leaving in a few days.

When he felt it was safe, he turned and watched her until she disappeared. He then leaned against the railing and looked at the ocean. He counted ten pelicans as they flew in formation, heading south in a perfect straight line. He admired their serenity, the simple pleasure—somehow evident to him—they seemed to draw from flying in unison. Was it Hegel who said that when you witness pleasure, you experience it?

When he returned to the hotel, the chambermaids were arriving for another long day, and yet they were cheerful, talking Spanish and laughing. The other day, when he came in from the back entrance through the parking lot, he noticed a couple of them arriving in what seemed like brand-new cars. He tried to imagine their homes, their neighborhoods, wondering if they came all the way from Miami or if they lived nearby.

He went up to his room and took a quick shower, deciding he'd have breakfast in the small French café a couple of blocks down Collins Avenue. He and Mary had lunched there and liked it. They sat outside, listening to Piaf and Brel, holding hands across the table. The owner-waiter, a Frenchman, lingered at their table and told them he had come to Miami Beach three years before. He had worked for a while as a waiter, then went on a six-month trek in Southeast Asia. When he returned a year ago, he opened the café with a couple of partners.

"Wow!" Mary had said, and the waiter smiled.

"Photography is my number one passion," he explained in his charming accent, "but in the meantime I have this…." He indicated the café. He told them he had studied law in Paris and had a law degree, but he couldn't find work, so he left France and came here to get a taste of America and to start a business.

"How does one come up with the cash to start a business?" Bruno wanted to ask, but didn't. Because he lacked the talent or the will, he always marveled at the courage and initiative of young people who took the risk and started their own business.

Just as he had envisioned it, the few tables on the small terrace were bathed in sunlight. He picked a table and, after a moment's hesitation, sat down with his back to the sun. The young owner was chatting with an older woman who had her poodle with her and was the only other customer at this hour. She sat in the shade under the awning. The waiter looked up, acknowledged Bruno with a nod, but took his time—the European way, Bruno thought with forbearance—coming over to take Bruno's order of coffee and croissant.

"And jam and butter, please," Bruno added.

"A *tartine*, then?" the owner asked, and Bruno, even though he wasn't exactly sure what the waiter meant by *tartine*, said yes. As far as he knew, *tartine* was toasted baguette. For a moment he worried that his croissant would arrive toasted, but then decided not to worry about it. Brel's *Ne me quitte pas* was playing, and Bruno's heart swelled with longing. Rose used to play Brel's albums throughout his childhood. High above, the sky was spotless and deep blue, fading into pale blue at the edges. Feeling mellow,

Bruno turned in his chair, raising his face to the sun and shutting his eyes.

"*Et voilà*," said the waiter, and Bruno, now alert, watched his muscular arms as they placed two white plates on the table, one holding his croissant—not toasted, he noted with relief—the other, two small silver containers of butter and jam. Next came the silverware, wrapped in a white cloth napkin, and finally his coffee, which the waiter poured into a cup from a French press, leaving it on the table for a refill. "*Quel service*," Bruno wanted to say, but he was worried it would come out wrong, even condescending.

"*Tartine*," Bruno said. "I thought it meant toasted baguette?"

"Oh," the waiter said, reaching for the croissant plate. "You want toasted baguette?"

"No, no." Bruno, too, reached for the plate. "I was just wondering what it meant. *Tartine*."

"It means you want butter and jam with your bread or with your croissant."

"I see. Thank you, it's perfect."

"Enjoy." The waiter turned, perhaps with an elusive French shrug, and went back to the woman and her poodle. Bruno sat up straight and proceeded to rearrange the plates to suit his customary pattern—coffee on the right, plates on the left—careful to do so in two casual motions so as not to appear overly fussy in the eyes of the poodle woman and the waiter.

Maybe, as Mary often grumbled, he *was* too fussy, too set in his ways, but it couldn't be helped. He liked things the way he liked them. The croissant was warm, and the coffee was strong and delicious. If he doesn't end up in Akumal, he could possibly establish a life for himself right here, a small, quiet life devoid of bothersome involvements and complications.

The poodle began to bark, and the woman bent down and spoke to it. "Why do you do that? I told you a million times not to do that."

Bruno smiled. If nothing else, he was a collector of human curiosities, quite a few of which were his own. Our lives, he mused, were chapters in other people's tales and daydreams. A lover, a neighbor, a friend—they all had their ideas about who you were and what you were about.

The owner-waiter crouched and patted the poodle's head; the poodle responded to his touch and quieted. Bruno wondered if the woman loved her dog or simply needed something to keep on a leash. She and her dog were probably regulars, maybe natives, maybe recent imports from somewhere else.

"We're all transient here," a woman had told him the other morning when he was coming back from the boardwalk and the two of them waited to cross Collins Avenue. She was complaining about the drivers going over the speed limit.

Bruno said, "Why doesn't someone complain to the authorities?"

"We're all transient here. No one cares enough to bother."

He opened his book at the marker. It was Mann's *Death in Venice*, perhaps not exactly the book to take on your first vacation trip with your lover, but he and Mary had watched the movie on cable a few nights before leaving New York. Mary yawned, turned on her side and fell asleep, but even though he had seen it before, he watched it till the end and, the next morning, looked for the book on his bookshelves. Now, rereading the book, he relived his kinship with Aschenbach. A certain passage in particular comforted him because he thought it described him perfectly:

"A lonely, quiet person has observations and experiences that are at once both more indistinct and more penetrating than those of one more gregarious; his thoughts are weightier, stranger, and never without a tinge of sadness. Images and perceptions that others might shrug off with a glance, a laugh, or a brief conversation occupy him unduly, become profound in his silence, become significant, become experience, adventure, emotion. Loneliness fosters that which is original, daringly and bewilderingly beautiful, poetic. But loneliness also fosters that which is perverse, incongruous, absurd, forbidden."

Indeed, Bruno thought, a tinge of sadness was present in him always. It was part of him, a sadness or a nostalgia he did not understand and could not explain, a sadness that was now momentarily relieved with Mann, a man who understood him so well, sitting next to him, reciting in a soft, thoughtful voice.

Mann spoke of his own experience, and the notion that Bruno's thoughts, like Mann's, were weightier and stranger than the common run, soothed him. He was troubled, however, by the idea that because he spent much of his time alone, his thoughts, trapped in his head, were as Mann said, absurd and perverse. He himself entertained that suspicion, but he never got far enough to arrive at a conclusion, which, at any rate, would have been impossible since the same process of looking inward would be involved in deciding whether or not what went on in his mind was absurd and perverse.

Moreover, trying to figure it out would have caused more confusion, thus confirming the futility of trying to fathom his mind or the mind of another. Even if the other were someone close, it was wiser not to assume he knew what was in their head.

Still, there was pleasure to be had in thought alone. Someone like him really didn't need company. Someone like him was better off alone, left alone to his thoughts, to his musings.

Besides, if he was down one day and up the next—in the end, what did it change and why did it matter?

Bruno raised his head. It took him a moment to adjust, but the one-legged woman was standing only a few feet away, smiling at the waiter who was pulling out a chair for her at the table of the poodle lady. The poodle was very excited, jumping at her knee, and she let go of a crutch and stroked its head. She sat down, placing both crutches under the table with meticulous care, one on top of the other. She was quite adept with them, as one who'd been using them for a while, and he wondered if she viewed them as a burden, a curse, or if she came to cherish them as part of herself. She wore a sundress of red and brown skinny vertical stripes, and he watched the strong ankle of her good leg and the white sandal on her foot—size eight, he guessed. He caught himself casually visualizing her stump as it rested on the seat, and instantly stopped, so as not to invade her privacy.

"Calm down, Pooch," the poodle lady said.

"That's all right, Linda. He's a dog, let him be."

Yes, Bruno agreed. Let him be.

"He's not a dog, Suzie. He's a person," Linda chided.

"Why, of course." Suzie laughed, and Bruno's flesh tingled. Suzie. So fitting. She could have been a Caroline—for some reason he foresaw a 'C' in her name—but the name Suzie, because surprising, added another dimension to her, a lightness alleviating the severity he had projected onto her. He wished to find the words to express his response to her name, to adequately describe the ringing clarity of her voice, of her laugh, without resorting to clichés, but the only association he came up with was a bell, as her voice and laughter reverberated across the open terrace. In response, he felt his eyes grow wide, like the eyes of a twelve-year-old boy eager for life and adventure.

The waiter had left and now came back and poured her coffee, and Suzie leaned forward and took a sip, then another. She leaned back in her chair and lit a cigarette, leisurely inhaling and blowing the smoke skyward.

A smoker! This, too, for some reason, delighted him. No food, he conjectured further, just black coffee and a cigarette for breakfast after a vigorous walk along the ocean. No doubt a creative person, an artist or a writer. And the mass of thick hair, the resolute nose and chin, the high, intelligent forehead, the long arms, the expressive hands. He felt a stir in his groin, and a helpless whimper escaped him. Fortunately, no one heard it except Pooch, who looked up and gave a short, questioning bark at Bruno.

"Pooch!" Linda said, then looked his way. Suzie turned to look, and Bruno, putting a smile on his face and thinking God bless you, Pooch, raised his hand in greeting. He saw a flicker in Suzie's eyes and knew she recognized him, but before he had a chance to make meaningful eye contact with her, the two women turned their heads.

This is a start, he thought. When I see her tomorrow—or maybe even sooner, maybe in the next minute—I'll say something. I'll talk to her, and she will have to respond.

Carrying a tray, the waiter appeared and placed a large plate before Suzie. So she did have breakfast, and a substantial one at that: a beautiful-looking omelet, with bright red cherry tomatoes and strips of lettuce. He watched as Suzie broke a piece of crunchy baguette and heaped a generous amount of butter on it.

Bruno licked his lips. Hearty appetite! He mouthed in her direction, and even though he had just eaten, he felt a sudden craving for an omelet and baguette. He motioned the waiter over.

"The check?" the waiter asked.

"No, no." He looked at Suzie's plate. "I want...." He pointed, and the waiter, puzzled, turned to look at Suzie then back at Bruno.

"Yes?"

"The omelet, please."

"Oh. The omelet?"

"Yes, please. What kind is it?"

"Fromage et jambon."

"Perfect," Bruno said.

Suzie ate fast and with obvious delight. He could only see her profile, but he had a clear view of her hands as she cut a piece of the omelet, laid it on the baguette, then bit into it, popping a cherry tomato into her mouth. When she chewed, she rested both hands on the table until she took a sip of coffee or picked up fork and knife for the next bite. She ate like an athlete, he thought, like someone who expends a lot of physical energy. The more he observed her, the more pleasant the act of observing became.

She grew in his mind. He admired the straight narrow bridge of her nose—the long, strong line, he thought, would be a painter's dream. It was not only perfect, but was also in perfect alignment with the high plane of her forehead and with the angular lines of her jaw and chin. Everything about her bespoke good health and confidence, the authority of an athlete, and Bruno recalled, with unease, Walter Winchell's epithet for Leni Riefenstahl: "Pretty as a swastika."

Linda was talking about a movie she had seen, and Suzie nodded but didn't speak. Something in her manner, something in her straight posture, told him she knew she was being watched. She slowed down, and offered Pooch a piece of baguette, and Bruno worried that his presence inhibited Suzie from fully enjoying her meal. He watched the mass of thick hair and let his tender musings drift toward her. *If you want me to, I'll get up and leave. Yes, I will. I don't want to leave, but if you want me to…. I'd do anything to please you, even though I'm not yet quite sure why I would want to please you. We could have dinner tonight. I know it's Christmas Eve, you probably have other plans, but might you consider including me?*

His omelet arrived, still sizzling, and Bruno, smiling with wonder and delight, put Mann in his jacket pocket. He had always loved omelets, and Rose's omelets were famous among his friends who came for sleepovers. Alexie, already a contrarian at the tender age of ten, had spurned his friends and the omelets that "stank up the house."

"Be careful, the plate is hot," the waiter said. "Would you like more coffee?"

"Please."

He spread a thin layer of butter on a piece of baguette, cut a strip of omelet and laid it on the baguette, then brought the offering to his mouth. Linda, he sensed, was looking his way while whispering something to Suzie. He wondered if they were friends, close friends, or just neighborhood acquaintances—Linda was a good thirty years older than Suzie. With her long, white-blond hair, her flowery shirt, and her silver bracelets, she looked like an old hippie. She had a large nose and the fierce, roving eyes of the persecuted.

The waiter came back and poured coffee into Bruno's cup, and Bruno nodded his thanks.

"Where is your wife this morning?"

Bruno nearly choked. "My wife?"

"She was with you a few days ago. You had lunch, I believe?"

"Oh, that." Bruno chuckled. "She's not my wife, she's a friend. She went back to New York."

"Ah." The waiter nodded. "Are you here on business?"

"No, no, just a short vacation."

"Christmas vacation?"

"Kind of, yes, Christmas vacation."

Alone? The question hovered between them, but the waiter didn't voice it. "Let me know if you need anything," he said and went back to Linda and Suzie. He leaned over and said something to Suzie. Suzie laughed her amazing laugh, then pushed her plate aside and lit another cigarette.

Bruno finished his omelet. He had quit smoking five years ago, but he could ask Suzie for a cigarette and puff on it without inhaling. This would be something, lighting up again after all these years. He was taking a big risk, but he could manage it. Just remember not to inhale. All he needed to do was summon his courage, go over to her, and ask for a cigarette. Better not to think about it too much. Better to just follow his instinct, his heart, and do it. Simple. Just do it. Stand up!

He stood up, his chair scraping the pavement, and the three at the table looked at him. Pooch barked.

"Stop it," Linda said to Pooch.

Bruno approached their table. "I'm sorry to bother you, but I was wondering if you…." Now he dared look at Suzie directly, right into her large, deep brown eyes. "I wonder if I could bum a cigarette."

She smiled at him, smoker to smoker. A prominent vein ran down the center of her forehead, and he worried it might pop. "I'm sorry," she said, picking up her yellow American Spirit pack and crushing it in her hand. "I'm out. There's a deli around the corner, they sell cigarettes."

"Oh," Bruno said, thinking fast. Should he tell her he wanted just one cigarette? He'd be happy to buy her brand and give her the pack, keeping one cigarette for himself.

"I have some in the kitchen." The waiter jumped to his feet. "No problem."

"Thanks." Bruno looked at Suzie, and she looked at him. His eyes traveled to her throat, so tan and smooth and vibrant. Good skin, he thought. Flawless.

The waiter returned and handed Bruno a pack of Marlboros. "Here, take it. I have more."

"I only need one," Bruno said.

"Take it, there are two in there, take it, I insist."

"Well, thanks." He stood there a moment longer, basking in their presence, then bowed a little bow and went back to his table. She could have invited him to join them, but she didn't. Still, she did look at him and even smiled. He took out a cigarette from the box and moved it under his nose, inhaling its aroma. The little white monster was back between his fingers—did he really want to do this? He could still put the cigarette back and throw away the pack or give it to a beggar or pretend to forget it on the table. And matches. He didn't have matches. He would have to get up again, go over to them—

"Here." The waiter materialized at his side with his lighter. "Out of everything, huh? No cigs, no lighter."

"Right." Bruno laughed and reached his cigarette to the flame. He drew on it and, like a veteran smoker, raised his head and inhaled, recalling, too late, his vow not to inhale. Then, mildly alarmed, he had to shut his eyes to counteract the momentary wooziness that overtook him. It wasn't unpleasant, but it felt new, nearly forgotten.

Look what I'm doing for you, Suzie. I'm smoking again.

He opened his eyes. Suzie fished in her pocket and handed the waiter a twenty dollar bill. She is leaving! He panicked, then calmed himself. He'll see her tomorrow on the boardwalk and then again right here at the café, where he would come for his breakfast, and she would, too. She reached under the table and stroked Pooch's head, Pooch yielding to her touch with obvious pleasure. She then picked up her crutches and stood up, steadying herself. She briefly glanced at Bruno, said "Ciao" to her friends, and whisked herself away. He wanted to turn and watch her until she vanished from view, but couldn't, not with the waiter and Linda watching.

His heart was pounding, and he took a deep breath, realizing, with a chilling astonishment, that his hands were shaking. The heart was a strong machine, he had read somewhere, but his heart was now delightfully weakened, and the thought hit him: I'm ready for love! Whatever organ in his body responsible for love— be it his brain, his heart, his penis—felt raw with anticipation. And if her missing leg shocked him at first, now he thought nothing of it. In fact, her handicap only reinforced his attraction to her. She was such a perfect creation, God himself felt he had to intervene and bring perfection down a notch. Every particle of hair and skin shone and sparkled, and she looked more radiant than all the Marys and Ellens put together.

When he paid his bill, he asked, casually, "Are you open tomorrow?"

The waiter said, "Of course, we're open every day, even on Christmas and New Year's."

"Great," Bruno said.

"Our customers demand it," the waiter explained with professional pride.

"I see. They come here every day?"

"That depends. Some do and some don't." The waiter smiled enigmatically, as if to indicate he had said all that he was going to say, but Bruno, stubbornly, continued to look at him, waiting for more.

"My mother," Bruno ventured, "is half French."

"Really. Do you speak it? French?"

"A little."

"Well." The waiter looked toward the kitchen. "I need to start preparing for lunch. We will see you again soon, yes?"

"Yes, you will," Bruno said.

He continued to sit. The sun was beating down on him, and he couldn't decide if he wanted to move to a table in the shade and read for a while or go back to the hotel. Linda was reading a newspaper, and Pooch was dozing on Suzie's now empty seat.

He had a whole day ahead of him. He could take the bus to Miami. Or he could go down to the beach and swim if the water is warm. He could walk the streets and look for Suzie. He could get on a plane and go back to New York, and so avoid spending Christmas alone in Florida.

Florida—the doomed state. A few weeks ago, he'd been sitting in a spacious Brooklyn living room, digesting a rich dinner and sipping Armagnac. Satiated, he was content to sit back and listen to the conversation of two other guests who were discussing the futility of antiwar demonstrations, and the clever strategy of a system that had abolished the draft, and so effectively got the mothers of America off its back.

Then one of the men suggested that Florida and California, due to climate change and ocean levels rising, might disappear off the face of the earth, and so rid the world of two imbeciles: Jeb Bush and Arnold Schwarzenegger.

Listening, Bruno's blood pressure began to rise, even as he told himself to keep his mouth shut. Clearly, the two peacocks were just showing off their colors, so why interfere? Let smugness rule!

"It doesn't help," he heard himself say. The men, who hadn't really included him in the conversation, now scrutinized him. "Division," he continued in what he considered a mild tone. "Intolerance."

"Yes?" one of the men said. He was smiling or smirking but the eyes behind the gold-rimmed glasses were hard.

"Well," Bruno, also smiling, said, "many people would die."

"Some people deserve to die."

"Oh." Bruno nodded, wishing he hadn't opened his mouth. All at once, the room went silent. The other guests, Mary among them, had stopped talking and were watching him and the two men.

"People die every day," the man continued, calmly crossing his legs. His fine leather boots gleamed with self-satisfaction.

"Indeed," Bruno said. "I do see your point. But why content yourselves with Florida and California? Why not New Jersey, Pennsylvania, Georgia? And the list, I'm sure, needn't stop there."

"No, it needn't. As far as I'm concerned, those too can go down the tube, and we may as well include Texas."

"And some parts of Brooklyn, too, I imagine," Bruno said, "as long as your corner of Cobble Hill is left intact."

"You imagine correctly," the man said, looking at the host and rolling his eyes.

"And I further imagine," Bruno continued, "that you and Jeb and Arnold may have something in common."

"Oh, *please*. Spare us."

Thankfully, the host intervened, recalling a joke involving God and organic chicken nuggets, and everybody laughed with relief, and Bruno, too, cracked a smile. The party continued more or less pleasantly but in the cab going home, Mary bristled. "So you managed to humiliate me and call attention to yourself yet again."

"They were jerks," Bruno said.

"Excuse me?! If there was a jerk in the room, it was you. You goaded them."

"No, my dear, they goaded me."

"They're my friends, not yours. You don't know them. All you had to do was keep your mouth shut."

"Really? So why even go out if I'm not allowed to open my mouth? Besides, believe me, I did try to keep the lid on it, but they were mindless and arrogant. I had to say something."

"They were just talking, for God's sake!" Mary glanced at the driver, who had just turned off his radio. She hesitated a moment, then went on, hushing her voice but still lecturing. "That's what people do in a dinner party. They talk."

Bruno, also aware of the driver, but too worked up to worry about it, and certain that the driver's solidarity rested with him, raised his voice. "What do you mean, 'just talking'? Words mean something, and, let me remind you, I, too, was 'just talking.'"

"They were joking, you moron, they didn't mean any of it."

"Moron. Thanks. Later you'll tell me it was just a word, you didn't mean it."

"No, I won't," she said, but weakly, retreating somewhat. "You sit there like a judge on his high chair and wait for someone to say something so you can pounce and contradict them. You do the same to me."

"Please. Can't you, for once, see it from my point of view? Why must you side with them rather than with me?"

"It's not a matter of siding with you or with them. We were invited to a dinner party, right? A dinner party in someone's home. You don't pick a fight with another guest. You don't like what someone says, you make conversation with someone else.

While the two of you decided to put your dicks on the table, the rest of us were discussing the real estate market."

"I don't care about the real estate market."

"You don't have to *care*, for Pete's sake. Just *listen*. You may learn something."

"I doubt it."

"God," Mary said, "you're impossible. I can't talk to you."

They were going over the Brooklyn Bridge now, and Bruno looked out the window, waiting for the uplift he usually felt when crossing it and sighting the awesome city at the edge of the water, its thousand lights burning holes in the dark. It was still grand, but ever since the towers fell, it never felt quite the same. Like most New Yorkers, he had taken the towers for granted, and only after they died he began to cherish them. There was an eerie elegance, he thought, a dignity in the way they went, each tower disintegrating, sinking into itself in a neat, economical fashion, as if wishing to minimize the devastation. During the hour or so they stood wounded, they became human to him, and as he watched on TV the lines of dark smoke dripping down their façades, he thought the towers were weeping, mourning the people they had sheltered. He also thought he saw reproach and condemnation of human folly in their black tears. What stabbed at his heart each time he came this way was not so much the physical absence as the instant recognition that somewhere among the buildings that made up the downtown cityscape there lay a pit, a black hole where three thousand everyday people had died a horrible death.

"Look at the view," he cajoled.

"I don't want to."

"Please." He touched her arm. "Let's be friends."

She pouted. "Not now. Maybe later."

Bruno sat up, startled. Where was he? On his bed, naked, and yet his skin felt hot, sweaty. After the shower, he must have turned off the air conditioner. The beginning of a headache was beating in his temples, disorienting him further.

He turned to look at the bedside table. Just then, the red digit tumbled from 5:56 to 5:57, and his heart, too, registered a beat. He lay back with a sigh. He shouldn't have taken a nap, not such a long one, especially after the snooze in the hammock by the pool, with a feverish Aschenbach chasing a chimera down the plagued alleyways of Venice, an enticing phantasm very much alive in his mind.

His friend Aschenbach. After the snooze, he'd come upstairs, took a shower, and then, seduced by the sun lovingly dappling the white duvet through the slanted blinds, he climbed onto the bed even as he told himself not to. He had meant to lie down for just a few minutes, and fell into a deep, two-hour sleep. Maybe he was even more exhausted than he knew—not so much physical exhaustion as mental, ever since Mary took flight as if he were a leper.

He should have known better. It was a mistake and immature of him and her to think they were a solid enough couple to set out on a two-week trip. They should have waited a little longer or planned a shorter trip. Maybe he had lost the habit of being with a woman or knowing how to please a woman day after day, twenty-four hours a day.

Maybe the two of them never truly connected. Maybe they clung to one another for the wrong reasons, hoping with time they would find a neutral zone where they could live together in peace.

He shifted screens in his mind and Suzie appeared, followed by Linda and Pooch, and soon the waiter and the delicious omelets he and Suzie consumed, albeit not together. In the end, he had left the café to go back to the hotel, but not before waiting a few seconds for Linda to notice him and possibly invite him to join her and Pooch. She did look up when he rose from the table, but then continued to read the paper, so he turned and left, relieved to enter the dim coolness of the hotel. He chatted a moment with the concierge, then crossed the lobby and went out to the pool area. Various types of the white and moneyed middle-class were lounging on the chairs, offering their wrinkles and fatty folds to the sun. Here and there, he noticed a Latino face and wished for himself the same skin, smooth and brown.

The guests relaxed by the pool, bronzing in the sun, and only he, the aimless professor, couldn't find rest. A woman lay topless on her stomach, the straps of her thong bikini cutting across her waist and down her buttocks. He watched the reddening, dimpled ass and asked himself if he wanted to lick or bite it, and, if yes, how badly.

He smiled. A few mornings ago he had managed to persuade Mary to go down to the beach rather than the pool, and as they sat on lounge chairs under an umbrella, two young girls in thong bikinis walked past, and Mary said, in her deliberate waspy intonation, "Well, what do you think of *that*?"

"Of what?" he asked, even though he knew she was referring to the girls.

"When you watch these nearly naked girls, what are you thinking?"

He looked at her, weighing his words carefully, wondering what she was driving at and whether jealousy was lurking behind the question, waiting to strike. "Nothing much. Nice to look at."

"Doesn't it make you think women are silly? Advertising their merchandise?"

He laughed. "Yes, maybe a little."

"And it doesn't bother you that you think that? That you think women are silly?"

"There's nothing wrong with being silly. Men are silly, too."

"But not as silly as women, correct?"

"I don't know, Mary. And why does it matter?"

"Because it does." Mary sat up, and Bruno felt a sudden contraction in his guts, as if he were wincing inside. "I can't stand it when women display how stupid and empty-headed they are."

Bruno looked at her, wondering what it would take to make a woman like Mary truly happy and accepting. He wanted to say that surely when she was these girls' age, she must have worn bikinis and miniskirts.

"Are you saying they shouldn't wear bikinis?" he asked.

"These are not bikinis, Bruno. These are a couple of nominal strings meant to draw the eye to specific body parts. They might as well be naked."

"I see what you mean," he said, keeping the peace. Mary was not exactly the cheerful type, but all her demons seemed to have broken loose in Florida. Maybe he had brought them out. He waited for her to say more, but she didn't. She took out her book and began to read, so he relaxed back and, secure behind his sunglasses, watched a woman to his left, who lay on a towel on the sand. She wore a black bikini and every so often raised a bronzed, sculpted arm and touched her hand to her skin, to her stomach, to her thigh—airy, absentminded caresses that captivated him and put him in a lull, until he heard Mary's voice, low and broken.

"You must think I'm a prude, an old, sour prude," and he, deeply touched, reached for her.

"No, never," he said, instantly forgetting the tan woman in the black bikini.

Still watching the reddening, dimpled ass and ruminating, he suddenly noticed two adolescent boys running along the pool deck and jumping in, screaming and splashing, tossing a beach ball between them.

Damn! he thought. He had hoped to get into the pool and swim a while. The boys, probably brothers, were both obese, and this angered him even more; already they seemed obtuse, and he blamed their mother, probably just as obese and obtuse.

Determined to enjoy himself, he went upstairs, changed into his bathing trunks, and went down again. As he descended the few steps into the pool, the boys stopped throwing the ball and watched him, perhaps already eyeing his head as a potential target. Let them dare, he thought, preparing for battle, then murmured, in his mother's calming voice: "Shush, Bruno. Cool it."

His mother. He must remember to call her later to wish her a Happy Chanukah and a Merry Christmas. He might even call Alexie, if only to talk to Gerry, her long-suffering, saintly husband, and ask after his nephews, whom he rarely saw, especially since they had left home for college. The last time he spoke to Alexie, she had been unusually mild, or maybe just tired. She had called him late one night to say she and Gerry would be leaving town for a few days, could he please come and feed the cats once a day, and he said that yes, he would be happy to, suppressing the urge to ask how come she was trusting him enough to do it right.

As far as he could remember, it was the first time she had ever asked for his help. Then she talked about a man who had been rude to her on the checkout line at the supermarket, and Bruno suggested something to the effect that if she tried to be more friendly and kept a smile on her face rather than a scowl, she might find that people were inclined to smile back.

"Most people," he said earnestly, glad that for once his sister was listening, "are eager to smile at others, are eager to make eye contact. Generosity begets generosity, you must know this?"

"No, I don't," she muttered, but the next day, going over to feed the cats, he found a note on the kitchen table thanking him for being patient with her, thanking him, in effect, for being the brother he was for her.

Bruno put on his goggles, carved for himself an imaginary lane, and began doing his laps. Once in a while, he peered at the boys and realized they were mindful of him, staying out of his path. So he was wrong about them. They were not obtuse at all, but polite, considerate. In fact, he was the obtuse one.

Swimming relaxed him. The back-and-forth generated a calming stillness in his head. Soon, Suzie appeared to keep him company, and he recalled the way her eyes shone up at him when he asked for a cigarette, the allure of her strong left ankle under the table, clad in a brown sandal. He wondered how she bought shoes, if she was required to purchase a pair, like everyone else, or if there were outlets that accommodated special needs. He thought it significant that she had opted not to avail herself of a prosthetic leg, and, from the way she carried herself, he concluded that she was defiantly proud of her handicap.

When he was done with his laps, he rested, leaning against the cool tiles at the edge of the pool. A woman strutted past, in her sixties, he judged, the straps of her bikini top under her arms, as if to say, I have no use for them, my breasts are still firm.

Indeed, they were, and she evinced the self-aware pride of an older woman who knew she was in good shape still and looked good for her age. Just then, one of the boys called out to him, asking if he wanted to play ball with them, and Bruno smiled and waved his arm, saying, "No, thank you, I'm out of shape."

"No, you're not, please, just for a little while," the boy pleaded, and Bruno, charmed, relented and joined their game until their mother arrived and said it was time for lunch. She was short and overweight, just as he had presumed, but he liked her smile, her diffidence. She seemed gentle and not obtuse at all.

Shame on him and his rotten state of mind—all thanks to Mary! He must and he will regain his composure and be restored to himself.

He got out of the pool and lay in the hammock in the shade, grateful for the light, pleasant breeze. He felt very comfy and at peace. The canvas hammock was wide and didn't pinch his skin. And when all the other guests, as if by command, rose to their feet, yawned, and went in for lunch, he was left alone to read his book in peace.

Obsessive, delirious Aschenbach was still chasing after his dream-boy through the hot and diseased alleyways of Venice, losing all sense of direction, following his bliss and his shame, the victim of the demon that would rob him of reason and dignity and lead him to the abyss. Poets, Aschenbach reflects, are like women for whom passion is exaltation, even madness—an all-consuming longing that must forever be for love and beauty.

Yes! Bruno, enchanted, looked up from the book. Indeed, beauty! Both divine and visible—according to Plato.

On the pool deck, a blackbird was pecking with quick, jerky motions at a packet of sugar under one of the vacated lounge chairs.

He tried to remember if he was ever obsessed with a woman he hardly knew, but the comfort of the hammock and the light breeze disallowed any taxing inquiries. He was content to just observe the bird and envision Mann, on one of his trips to Venice, encountering the boy he so vividly portrays in the book. In fact, Mann had said as much in one of his letters, and Mann's wife, years later, confirmed there had been such a boy. It was, therefore, likely that Mann had actually followed the boy one afternoon, just as he describes it in the book, but it was just as likely that Mann had dared in fancy what he couldn't or wouldn't in real life. And so, entering Aschenbach's inflamed psyche, Mann had put himself through the humiliation and exhilaration of chasing after his dream, all the while recognizing the futility of such a pursuit and the inevitable dissolution.

It wasn't idle curiosity—Bruno told himself—that moved him to speculate about Mann. It was more a matter of wanting to get closer to the man himself, to the flesh and blood Thomas Mann, to be intimate with him and to know, *feel*, what life was like for him. The exalted state of madness was not the province of women and poets alone. Any man, given the right circumstance, could just as readily propel himself into the void.

The ever-tempting oblivion. The seduction and allure of what lay beyond and yet within reach if one gave in to it. What was life if not the fortitude to follow the liberating dictum of the gargantuan Rabelais, *fay çe que vouldras.*

Bruno resumed reading, but soon the gentle swing of the hammock, the light breeze, and the occasional call of a bird, invited him to let go. His eyelids grew heavy, and he allowed himself to drift away. How calm he felt. How purely physical, heavy, and yet light, cradled in the hammock. Nothing mattered. He was floating in space, his heart and mind in perfect sync. His arms resting at his sides, it was possible he was actually levitating—such perfect equilibrium! He walked in the field and saw in the distance a stooped figure clad in white. The figure beckoned to him, and he quickened his step and walked into his father's open arms, an incredible feeling of peace engulfing him.

What a vision—Bruno, remembering, now shifted on the bed. It was rare his father visited him in a dream. He had awakened from the dream and remained in the hammock until the guests, heavy with food, returned from their lunches and flopped themselves onto the lounge chairs around the pool.

Bruno looked at the clock again. Now the red digits showed 6:03, and even though it felt good to just lie there and listen to his thoughts, his spine and limbs sinking deeper and deeper into the mattress, he forced himself to rise.

Funny thing about the body: the more you give it—food, sleep—the more it wants. Give it little, and it demands little.

In the bathroom, on the counter, he noticed a couple of blond hairs—Mary's, no doubt—which somehow escaped the maid's notice. He wiped the counter with a tissue and flushed it down the toilet. He rinsed his mouth, swallowed two aspirins to kill his headache, and walked out to the balcony to gauge the temperature and decide what to wear. He stood there, naked, enjoying the freedom to stand there naked and take in the coolish night air. All the other balconies were dark. Still, he wondered if someone was watching him from behind a curtained window. Probably not. It was Christmas Eve, nearly dinnertime. He turned and went back into the room to get dressed.

He crossed Collins Avenue. At his own peril, he thought with mirthless fatalism, even though he had the light. But the green light lasted only a few seconds before the red stop-hand began flashing its warning. No wonder the older people here seemed terrified when crossing—would they make it to the other side in time? There was a large button on a pole for pedestrians to press, which he and Mary soon stopped pressing when they realized it had no effect whatsoever on the traffic light. The stream of cars continued to flow, and pedestrians stood waiting for a good three or four minutes no matter how often and how furiously they pressed the button.

He reached the boardwalk and walked north. It was evening. The winter sun had set, and the round, attractive lamps along the boardwalk gave off a bright, reassuring light. The ocean was calm and dark. It was green during the day, with the sun shining upon it, the soft green of grapes. Two huge cruise ships were perched on the horizon, their fairytale lights ablaze. He imagined the passengers in their cabins, especially the women, dressing up for dinner, then perhaps some dancing. It was Christmas Eve, their spouses were nearby, and the starched and uniformed crew of a luxury liner would make sure they had a good time.

He went past two well-dressed men who walked leisurely, hands in pockets, discussing a friend who had gone to California for her mother's funeral. They were gay, he thought, but then perhaps not. Perhaps they were two husbands out for an evening stroll while their wives got ready in their homes or in their hotel suites. They seemed relaxed, comfortable in their dinner jackets, in their solid middle-age, and Bruno admitted to himself he envied them.

Three young girls ran along the beach, calling and laughing. A couple of homeless men sat on a bench, sharing a bottle in a brown paper bag, and Bruno, wondering if Wild Irish Rose was a favorite here as it was in New York, envied them, too. As he went past them, he heard one of them say, "We can kill each other, but we can't respect each other," and Bruno agreed.

He then thought about dinner. He wasn't very hungry, but he might go to the French café and have something, maybe an appetizer. Or he might decide just to scan the tables, hoping to find Suzie. It was unlikely she would be there, but he could go and just have a look, then turn around and go back to the hotel. True, he was alone, but he could watch TV, or read, then fall asleep. Another day and night of his dwindling life. Christmas notwithstanding. On the other hand, if he did find Suzie at one of the tables, he wouldn't hesitate a moment...

Bruno smiled, heaving his chest and drawing in a long, deep breath. He would not allow himself to plunge into fantasy or despair. If she was there, fine. And if she wasn't, that was fine too. He hardly knew her, and he'd be going back to New York in a few days. Although, if he really wanted to, if he had a reason to, he could extend his stay here. He had no classes, no real commitments, until mid-January.

In the tall condominiums, Christmas trees blinked in living rooms, and quite a few of the balconies were festooned with small, cheerful lights.

Mary. Suzie. Could they have been more different? If there was a God up there, allowing Bruno free will in a preordained framework, what was that God thinking? Did He have a plan? Was there logic? Did reason prevail at the end of the tunnel? He and Mary had planned to spend Christmas here, in snowless Miami Beach, but for the first time ever, he would be spending it alone, which would be all right unless, by some miracle, he'd meet Suzie at the café.

He looked at his watch: 7:09. He'd been walking for about twenty minutes. He turned on his heels and began to walk back. The two cruise ships, which were near each other when he first saw them, were now far apart. The oval-shaped one was farther away and seemed very small—a distant island, its lights blinking in the enormous darkness. The rectangular ship, still near, resembled a long, stationary bus, and Bruno supposed it was one of those gambling ships that went out a ways and docked for a few hours before heading back to shore. One day, he thought, he might board such a ship, spend time on the deck and, like a convalescent, take in lungfuls of ocean air. He imagined Mary at Joyce's festive table and wondered if she thought of him at all. If she did, did she recall a good or a bad moment?

Usually, the two of them found momentary peace when Mary sat in his lap or they cuddled up on the couch and watched TV, adding their commentary to the day's events. But even such peaceful moments sometimes erupted into a storm, as happened a few nights before their scheduled flight to Miami. This should have been yet another sign, but the two of them had elected to ignore it, possibly because it was just another fight, or the fact that canceling the trip would have been more of a hassle than taking it. Besides, they both needed a break. Both wanted to get out of the city and enjoy a few days in the sun.

Before the fight, they had been lying on the couch, tight and cozy, watching the late night news, when the newscaster said the most banal thing he repeated every night: "And now a look at our exclusive forecast."

Mary scoffed. "Exclusive forecast."

"Well, it's their own exclusively paid forecaster."

"It's their way of hyping everything, even the weather,"

Still in good humor, he said, "No need to take it so seriously, it's their job."

Mary pulled away from him and stood up. "You don't get it, do you? You always do this. You never really *listen* to what I'm saying. You must always, *always*, contradict me."

Slightly baffled and also a bit miffed, he said, "I wasn't contradicting you. I was just responding to what you said."

"Exactly!" she said, then went to the bathroom and slammed the door. He listened for sounds, but none came. What was she doing in there, hiding?

Frustrated, he turned off the TV and was about to get up and go knock on the door, when she reappeared.

In a quiet, controlled voice, she said, "You see, we can't even have a civilized conversation about something as trivial as the weather. This should tell us that something is the matter, it doesn't work. It can't work. Something deeper is going on, something we're both unaware of."

He didn't share her view. He didn't think something deeper was going on, not deeper, at any rate, than two people trying to adjust to living as a couple, but he was glad she had included herself as part of the problem rather than placing all the blame on him. "Like what?" he asked.

"Like, I don't know. I just said I didn't know, didn't I?"

He nodded, suddenly deflated, yet in self-defense, his mind groped for an opening that would lead to clarity and peace.

"Why don't you help me out?" she asked.

Exasperated, he thought his brain was about to explode. "Well, Mary, I wish I could. I wish I knew how. I think we're both high-strung. I also think I should be more understanding."

She crossed her arms. "More understanding of what?"

He felt a tickle in his nose. It was comic the way Mary, his inquisitor, stood there, arms crossed, belligerent, and yet oddly needy, as if waiting for him to say just the right words, words she needed to hear before letting both of them off the hook. His lips twitched as if stifling a hysterical urge to laugh.

"I think you're right." He shifted on the couch, still battling hysterics. "Maybe something is fundamentally wrong."

"Like what?"

"Like maybe you're bored with me," he offered. "Maybe I don't satisfy your needs."

"So where do we go from here?" she asked.

"I don't know." Interesting, he thought, how she had turned the conversation so he would be the one to verbalize a problem that, if it existed at all, she initiated. And now, he thought further, she was leading him to the point where he would suggest a separation he didn't want.

"Well, think about it," she said and sat in the armchair.

He leaned forward. "You think about it."

"Let's both of us think about it."

He smiled. "Don't you think it's a bit absurd? This non-conversation we're having? Maybe I shouldn't have said what I said about the forecaster. Frankly, I don't even remember what I said, but we all say silly things that mean nothing. Why dwell on it?"

"I agree," she said, "but the fact that we do dwell on it means something, and we should explore it."

She is bored, Bruno thought. Or insecure, needing me to reassure her. "I have no complaints," he said, "so it must be coming from you, You're dissatisfied with me, that's quite clear."

"And?"

"And I don't know. It's up to you. If you have some specific complaint, please tell me and I'll try to correct it. It's never my intent to offend or to hurt you."

She observed him, her green eyes steady, unblinking.

"Hmmm," she said, and then as if a new spirit had taken over her, she gave him one of her delicious smiles. A feeling of forgive-and-forget washed over him, even as the thought crossed his mind that he was a fool, allowing her to manipulate him this way and that. He recalled something he had read long ago about how decent and loving men fell for the slightest sign of affection, even when they suspected the person showing them affection was, in fact, shrewdly feeding them what they craved.

"Come." He patted the couch, and Mary, like a leopard, approached the couch and landed in his lap. She was warm and soft, and he parked his hand between her thighs. A moment later they were watching TV again, reconciled—but, for Bruno, also disconcerting—as if nothing had happened.

All at once he realized he was alone on the boardwalk, and he quickened his step. He was a stranger here, a tourist. Maybe the boardwalk wasn't safe after dark. He heard footsteps behind him and, unable to stop himself, turned around to look. It was a woman in her thirties or forties wearing a dark jogging suit. She wasn't jogging. She was walking fast, the water swishing in the bottle attached to her waist. It was a good habit, he thought, to carry water with you. Maybe if he decides to stay a little longer, he would adopt it.

The woman passed him, and he watched her buttocks. She had a strange way of walking, as if deliberately sashaying, and he remembered Alexie who had been told by a doctor she should sashay more because it was good for the spine and hips. He must remember to call them, Rose and Alexie. If he didn't feel up to it tonight, then tomorrow, first thing.

The sashaying woman disappeared into one of the side lanes, and he was alone again but no longer concerned about his safety. Where did all the Hasids go? Christmas meant nothing to them, so why weren't they out walking? Maybe it was the first night of Chanukah, and they were seated around the large table, partaking of the customary holiday dishes, talking about the heroic deeds of the Maccabees and singing Chanukah songs. Much later, when the table had been cleared, they would recite *Birkat Hamazon*.

A Hasid family, he knew, was a cohesive unit centered on the calendar, the community, and the kitchen table. In addition to the major holidays, there were feasts and celebrations having to do with a wedding, with the new bride and groom, and with childbirth, not to mention the festivities welcoming the Sabbath Queen who came around every Friday evening.

It was Moses, Bruno's father told him, who had given the gentiles their shopping weekend. For the Jews, it was a day devoted to God and family. Moses, the first Socialist, had gone to Pharaoh, demanding he grant his Hebrew slaves a day of rest on the Sabbath. God, too, had rested from His work on the seventh day. The Hebrew word for the Sabbath, Bruno's father explained, was *Shabbat*, derived from the root verb that meant to cease work.

When Bruno and Alexie were growing up, their father wished to keep the Jewish traditions present in their lives. They celebrated all the holidays, and the Friday night meal was sacred: no TV, no radio, no excuses. The family sat down together to welcome the Shabbat with songs.

Over the years, Bruno sometimes found himself telling close friends he was glad his father had exposed him to religion and to prayer. True, he no longer practiced or went to *shul* on a regular basis, but the essence was still there, alive in him.

Soothed by his thoughts and the blessed memory of his father, Bruno took the side lane that led to Collins Avenue. A bearded man, a beatific expression on his face, sat on a bench, his face turned upward to the trees and sky as if listening to a divine symphony. So, he wasn't all alone or special in his aloneness. Here was another man, beatifically solitary on Christmas Eve.

He crossed Collins Avenue and walked the few blocks to the French café. A small light shone in the kitchen window, which gave him hope, but the terrace was dark and empty. He approached the kitchen door and peered inside. A young man in a white apron stood leaning against the stove, smoking a cigarette.

"Hello," Bruno said, and the man nodded.

"Are you open tonight?" Bruno asked, even though the answer was plain to see.

The man, a tight smile on his lips, shook his head no.

"Well, thank you anyway."

Bruno turned and walked away, feeling numb. Why did the owner lie to him, saying they would be open tonight? Or maybe the owner was just having his bit of fun with him, and he, fool-ishly and pathetically focused on seeing Suzie again, hadn't caught on.

An hour later, he was in his room devouring a cheeseburger and fries he had ordered from room service, watching *Annie* on TV. A red rose in a small glass vase came with the burger, and Bruno asked the waiter if the rose was a customary gesture or a special addition for the holiday. The waiter smiled the way immi-grants who don't know the language very well smile, so Bruno smiled back and tipped him handsomely.

Now, hunched over the plate, he sat and ate, finding comfort in the fact that many millions across America were watching *Annie* with him. He had hoped to catch a French movie where food would be served, so he could share a meal with the characters on the screen and bite into a crunchy baguette, a wedge of Camem-bert, and other delicacies, but instead he got *Annie*. He had managed to avoid seeing the movie for years, and couldn't believe he was actually watching it now in a hotel room in Miami Beach.

All the same, he was watching it, even finding solace and sim-ple wisdom in the refrain, "Tomorrow, you're always a day away." And, on second thought, it made perfect sense that he was watch-ing a movie he would never have watched in his normal life. In a way, a vacationer was a kind of detainee, removed from his sur-roundings and his everyday life.

When he finished his meal, he remembered the one cigarette he still had in the pack and, after a moment of pretending to resist the temptation, he poured himself a whisky and lit the cigarette, welcoming the pleasant wooziness in his head.

After *Annie,* he watched another movie, this one about a mom dying of breast cancer. She is diagnosed around June, makes it through Christmas Eve, and dies on Christmas Day. After agonizing and heartrending scenes in hospital, she is allowed to go back home to take part in the holiday festivities with her family. Now and then, Bruno reached for the napkin and wiped a tear.

Hollywood producers, it seemed, were enamored of stories about moms dying of cancer on or around Christmas. No mom ever died on Chanukah or Rosh Hashanah, yet many of the producers and the screenwriters were Jewish. Was there something about Christmas and Christianity that made death so beautiful and moving?

After the cancer movie, he watched the Shopping Channel and learned that women had to have a purse not so much for the practical use of carrying their lipsticks and keys, but more so as yet another weapon in their arsenal of eye-catching accessories.

"It's like catching sight of a butterfly," the woman on TV said. "The right accessory and a bright color will catch *his* eye. Shape and color are all that matter."

Finally, around midnight, he turned off the TV and, with a sigh, punched the pillows and rested his head. He berated himself for having watched TV instead of reading Mann, but, he didn't do this very often, and it did make the night easier to bear.

Easier to bear and, as the song promised, tomorrow was only a day away. Tomorrow he will see his Suzie, but now he needed to get some rest. He felt himself drifting, hovering on the precipice of blessed oblivion, when the theater in his mind came alive, and images of the dying mother from the movie, intermingled with images of Mary and Suzie, began to agitate under his lids. He sought to create a lull in his mind by taking small, nearly imperceptible breaths, hoping to trick his brain and slink under into a delicious darkness. He'd never learned how to meditate and had no mantra, so he repeated the word "mantra," but to no avail.

It was going to be one of those nights when his brain went on a fishing expedition, seeking out and alighting on sore points. Bits of dialogue, real and imagined, kept repeating in his head as he found himself arguing with someone, trying to prove a point, or when not arguing, shining a spotlight on himself telling a story, and as he watched himself telling an especially moving story— usually the life story of his father, a story he could never bring himself to actually share with another living soul—his eyes would fill with tears, and he would have to stop, never able to finish the story.

Bruno turned over onto his side. Why, why did he even bother to press his point of view? What was it that drove him to argue with people over politics, personal issues, and other quibbles? Why couldn't he have pleasant, rather than contentious, conversations going on in his head? And now, to add to his misery, his next door neighbors, two Russians, had come back from their night on the town. They were obviously drunk, speaking loudly, shouting in spite of the late hour. The fact that they could be so inconsiderate infuriated him.

Vanity, it is all vanity, said King Solomon, the wisest of men, but the Hebrew word for vanity, *hevel*, also meant vapor, the hot air that issued from our mouths with our breaths. This is what humans amounted to, hot air. In addition to *hevel*, he had grown up with: "The thing that hath been, it is that which shall be; and that which is done is that which shall be done: and there is no new thing under the sun"—yet another nihilistic pearl from King Solomon, whom Bruno's father, during quiet reflective moments, was fond of quoting. King Solomon and the Carpathian Mountains, lovingly described by the father and lovingly embedded in the son's mind.

Maybe the two Russians would soon tire and fall asleep, Bruno hoped. Maybe he was a lacking human being. Why couldn't he take joy in the joy of others? He could. But not when he was trying to sleep.

He recalled the first time he experienced a cat's rough tongue. Whose cat was it? He couldn't remember. He was well into his thirties, and he reached a hesitant hand to his friend's cat, even though he hadn't been too fond of them, and the cat sniffed and licked his hand, which he found it startlingly agreeable.

His neighbors continued with their racket. He considered calling the reception desk to complain, then decided he'd better take care of it himself. Why get his neighbors in more trouble than was necessary? From the sound of it, it was just the two of them. They hadn't brought back women, as one might have expected. He got out of bed, threw on some clothes, and walked out of the room, remembering to take his key just in case the door shut behind him. To his surprise, their door was ajar the length of the security chain, and he glimpsed one of them, the tall one he had seen earlier when he came back from the pool. He was sitting on one of the beds with his back to the door. His friend, chubby and bald, stood laughing at the far end of the room. A pack of cigarettes sat at the center of the empty bed, and the idea flashed in Bruno's mind that he could ask for a cigarette and so make friends rather than complain.

"Please be quiet," Bruno heard himself say in a voice much harsher than he had intended. He sounded stern and old, an old miser, a fool. Embarrassed by his own voice, he quickly turned to go back into his room, but he did hear the tall one mumble something that sounded like an apology, while the other, the chubby one, called out to him, "Do you have ice?"

"No!" Bruno barked and slammed his door for emphasis.

Of course, there was an ice machine at the end of the hallway, but if they couldn't remember this in their inebriated state, he was not going to assist them and so encourage them to continue drinking and shouting till morning.

His heart pounded. Through the wall, he heard them laugh the happy, carefree laughter of the young and unconscious. Only a few years ago, he thought, I was just like them. Especially after a few drinks. Why not be tolerant? Angry, more at himself than at them, he pulled off his clothes and climbed back into the bed.

The two Russians grew quiet. Good! Bruno smiled, but with no feelings of malice toward them. A few minutes later, he heard them leave, probably in search of ice. He'd better hurry and fall asleep before they got back.

Desperate, he massaged his left earlobe, as he used to do for Ellen, hoping what had worked for her would work for him. Women, he reflected with forbearance, had small, shrewd ways of endearing themselves to men. Ellen, on nights she couldn't fall asleep, would ask him to massage her earlobes, sometimes even waking him, and he, no matter how tired, would comply, and she would moan and purr, saying he had magical hands. And indeed, within five minutes, she'd be fast asleep. He wondered if, at this very moment, Ellen's new husband was massaging her earlobes, and if Ellen was moaning and purring, telling him he had the touch.

He massaged his left earlobe, then his right, but nothing helped. His febrile brain kept racing, no way was he going to fall asleep.

Enough! He jumped out of bed. He had only one life to live, so he might as well live it like his neighbors, now roaming the streets in search of ice. He got dressed and went into the bathroom, bringing his face close to the mirror. He looked tired, even haggard. Did he really want to go out to the dark uncertainty of the streets? What would he be looking for? Why not just stay in and try to sleep? Or read? On close inspection, his lips seemed to be thinning, losing definition, so he stretched his mouth wide and sort of grimaced, showing his teeth, even the crown on the upper right side. Maybe he should stay in and go to bed like any normal adult.

No. He bent over the sink and splashed cold water on his eversuffering and enduring face. There. More human now.

The lobby was empty and quiet, except for the lonely echoing sound of his soles, squeaking unpleasantly the length of the shiny terrazzo floor. Of course, he was wearing the wrong kind of shoes. Why didn't he insist on packing the sandals he had bought in Akumal? Because Mary, dear Mary, did not approve of sandals as appropriate footwear for men. Men had large feet and ugly toes, she claimed. Not exactly an appetizing sight.

The drowsy clerk at the reception desk looked up, somewhat alarmed. "Can't sleep," Bruno explained, and the clerk, perhaps fearing that Bruno—yet another tiresome guest—would engage him in conversation, kept a blank expression on his face.

Don't worry, Bruno said silently, I won't bother you. He reached the door, then thought of something and walked back to the clerk.

"Is it safe to walk out this late?" he asked in a flat, frosty tone, and the clerk, finally remembering to activate his smile muscles, smiled. "Oh, sure, no problem."

"Thanks." He didn't quite believe the clerk, but he had made up his mind to go for a walk, and walk he would. Instantly, the dark sky soothed him, the fresh air soothed him, and he filled his lungs. Yes, he was alive, he was healthy, and for all his thoughts about death, he might still be around for a while. Briefly, he was inclined to feel sorry for himself—alone on Christmas Eve—but then decided it was silly. What did Christmas Eve mean anyway?

It was just another night like all the others. Except as occasions for familial gatherings, holidays no longer meant much to him, so why be bothered about it now?

He turned right on Collins Avenue, deciding to walk toward Lincoln Road. Now his steps echoed on the sidewalk, but not unpleasantly. Here and there, a faint light beckoned in a window behind a gauzy curtain. Miami Beach seemed a ghost town, and he was the only ghost walking. Except for a car or two, there was no traffic, the sky was clear, and the night air was crisp, all of which combined to lift his spirits, validating this seemingly irre-sponsible excursion into the dark and strange streets, giving him courage to continue. It was good that he was alone, free to roam and follow his whims. If Mary were here, the two of them would probably be asleep, dead to the world, and he wouldn't be expe-riencing the beauty of this late-night walk.

No question, it was better this way. He depended on no one, and no one depended on him, even if he still enjoyed rare mo-ments of grace when he would be sitting with friends, and the realization would hit him that he was fortunate to be in their com-pany. During such moments, doubts and apprehensions left him, only to come back later. Doubts and apprehensions had become a part of who he was, but he was reluctant to share them with others, unwilling to reveal his growing vulnerability, due, no doubt, to the demoralizing fact of aging.

Human nature being what it was, he was sure to gain a friend's empathy for as long as the confession and the drinks lasted, but that same empathy would later breed its opposite, a kind of condescension or pity which would always shimmer between him and the friend, who even might, when the need arose, use against him the very words of despair that he volunteered.

Indeed, a Yiddish saying had become his guide: Spare me your sting, and you can keep your honey. He who was your friend today might be your enemy tomorrow, spouses and children included. And so, necessarily, one kept to oneself, offering the world a mirage, the shadow of a phantom.

We are all phantoms—Bruno welcomed this nocturnal thought. When we accept that no one can know us, that we cannot know others, only then is real peace attainable.

As if from nowhere, two women, tall and slender in their exquisite, white silk dresses, appeared a few steps ahead of him. Bruno's eyes and heart lit up. They had long dark hair and seemed quite flamboyant, both sporting a flowing black scarf around their shoulders. One of them wore a green hat with a long feather shooting up from it. As he watched them totter on their very high heels, wondering why they even bothered with high heels, it suddenly dawned on him that they were men. Only drag queens dared take femininity to such baroque extremes. He quickened his step, thinking he might talk to them, be friendly and say hello, but when they reached the corner, they got into a waiting car and sped away.

Too bad, Bruno thought, turning right into Lincoln Road. Here, too, all was dark and all the restaurants were closed, he was the only lunatic walking the streets. Here and there, he saw a shadowy figure against the wall, possibly a homeless man or a drunk. Miami Beach, he knew, could be sleazy, and as he told himself to be alert, an excitement tinged with fear mounted in him, perhaps the same excitement and fear that had animated Aschenbach in his pursuit, an anxious anticipation of what was to come.

He went past the Italian restaurant, then took the first right, and there it was, Snow White, just like the waiter had promised. A small neon sign in the shape of a mermaid blinked its welcome. The mermaid seemed to be swinging her hips at him, and yet she looked virginal, her impish smile sweet and inviting.

Strange how his legs led him here to this cute mermaid. Or perhaps not so strange, since it was one of the few destinations he knew about in this part of town.

He heard footsteps and, startled, turned around. A man and a woman were walking fast toward him, and before he had time to move out of their way, they split and went past on either side of him into the club, the woman smiling at him over her shoulder, as if amused by his hesitant loitering near the door.

Did he really want to go inside?

No, not really, but, he had come all this way, he might as well go in. Why not? He had nothing to lose except time. He'd have a couple of drinks, then head back to the hotel.

He pulled the door and entered a dark, cavernous space. A mock-up Malebolge, he mused, recoiling instinctively.

Not his kind of place. If he had an idea what a dungeon might look like, this was it. The raw and sloping concrete floor, the stale odor of beer and cigarette smoke, the dim lights. And he felt certain everything he touched would be grimy, sticky. But not yet a hundred percent sure he wanted to leave, he remained standing near the entrance, adjusting to the semi-darkness.

The interior looked anything but virginal or snow white. The walls were painted black, and the small red lamps on the tables along the walls were the only source of light. A few patrons sat at the tables and along the bar. To his right, he now noticed, stood a small stage, and two muscular men in T-shirts and jeans were setting up the sound system.

Maybe it's not so bad, Bruno reconsidered. A performance of some kind would soon begin, and he was here already. He might as well let himself experience whatever the place had to offer.

He approached the bar and sat down on a stool in the center. The bartender, a tall, anorexic-looking blond, her short hair spiked, came over and in a low, indifferent voice asked what was his pleasure.

A Brit. Charming accent and intonation. And super modern, too, flat-chested, and the usual tattoos and piercings, including a couple of studs on her bottom lip and over her one eyebrow. The other eyebrow had been shaved. How did one even approach such a woman? he wondered. The serpentine silver lettering on her white T-shirt read: Snow White, and Bruno felt himself smile.

She was still standing there, looking at him with her strange, slightly slanted cat eyes. She had a great comic strip face, sharp and angular, and he realized he had yet to tell her his pleasure. He thought he might have a beer, which he could drink directly from the bottle and so avoid drinking from a glass, but then heard himself say, "Scotch, please," and she asked if Dewar's was okay, and he said that yes, Dewar's was okay. Ice? No, no ice, he said, recalling his Russian neighbors roaming the streets for ice.

They should come here, Bruno thought, his head bobbing on his neck with cocky self-contentment. Yes, it was a good idea to come here and be a part of something alive and happening. He felt his heart beating. Mary, naturally, would never dream of stepping into such a place, but he was different, more open, more adventurous. Mary, in fact, was limited and narrow-minded, whereas he could appreciate an occasional taste of the darker side of life. He had liberated himself. Consciously or subconsciously he had driven her away and so reclaimed his freedom.

Buoyed by his thoughts and with a fresh drink before him, he felt more and more that he belonged right where he was. The young men on stage were testing the mike, which meant that someone would soon be singing, maybe bawdy songs to go with the atmosphere.

He downed his drink and ordered another, and by the time she brought it to him, he had worked up the nerve to ask her name—Celia, she said—and then, with a boyish timidity, he asked for a cigarette, pointing at a pack he had noticed on the counter. Celia smiled, as if she had been expecting him to ask for one, and handed him the pack with a lighter on top of it.

"Take as many as you need," Celia said, leaving the pack on the bar.

American Spirit, he noted, just like Suzie's. He helped himself to one and inhaled deeply, reflecting that he had been wrong about Celia. She was welcoming, tattoos and piercings and all, and pleasant to watch. Maybe she wasn't a woman at all. She could just as easily be a man. These days it was sometimes hard to tell, especially on a night like tonight. It was late, long past his bedtime, and the smoky room and the dim red lights could make one doubt that anything was knowable, and, at any rate, who cared. He was a tourist, sampling life in foreign surroundings, allowing himself to do what normally he wouldn't have occasion to do.

See? Already he was working on his third drink and smoking his second cigarette. He was living the life. The life he had denied himself for too long, focusing on work, discipline, and restraint. Such folly! Discipline and so-called healthy living.

All at once he noticed that to his left, at the far end of the bar where it rounded toward the wall, a woman was sitting with her back to the bar. He couldn't see her face, only her straight back, but something in the way she held herself told him she was at-tractive. She was possibly the owner, sitting on a high stool that looked like a throne, much more comfortable than the stool he was sitting on, which had no back to lean against. She was wearing the same tight T-shirt as Celia, and the more he watched her, the more he thought he knew her. There was something familiar in the way her hair fell to her shoulders, in the way she kept her back straight while leaning slightly forward. Then he heard Celia call, the woman turned, and his eyes met hers, and he nearly fell off his stool.

Suzie! He wanted to shout. Suzie! What are you doing here?

She, too, seemed surprised to see him, but soon she smiled and, with an imperceptible nod of her head, invited him to join her. He seized his drink in one hand and Celia's cigarettes and lighter in the other and walked over, a bit wobbly on his feet. The woman Suzie had been talking to rose and walked toward the stage, and Bruno, with a start, now recognized her as one of the two transvestites he had seen on the street.

"Oh." In his confusion, he pointed at the departing figure with his drink, spilling some of it on his wrist and the floor. "I know her. I saw her on my way here. There were two of them."

"Two of them!" Suzie laughed, pointing at the vacated seat. "Didn't your mother tell you it's not polite to point?"

"I'm sure, many many years ago," Bruno said, sitting down and finally facing her. "Funny you should mention my mother," he said, forgetting what he was about to say.

"Why funny?"

"Because. Because I think you remind me of her, maybe."

Suzie observed him. "Your mother? You're kidding."

He shook his head, which suddenly felt heavy. "No, no kidding. Is she a friend of yours?" he asked, this time refraining from pointing, but looking in the direction of the stage.

Suzie smiled. "That's Nicole, and yes, she's one of our regular performers."

Bruno nodded, holding his tongue. The prurient side of his nature desired to have a short discussion about the she being a he, not that it mattered, of course, he'd add, and so on, but he sensed that Suzie would not cooperate. "What kind of performance?" he asked.

"Lip-synching. She's one of the best, and tonight it's going to be Christmas carols."

"Really?" he said, sipping the last of his drink. He thought it kind of grotesque—lip-synching in general and lip-synching Christmas carols in particular—but then thought better of it. What else to do on Christmas Eve than sing Christmas carols and get everyone in the holiday spirit, even here in dark and seedy Miami Beach.

He laughed. "Holiday spirit."

"After a fashion," Suzie said, and he thought he detected scorn in her voice. She looked at his cigarettes and lighter. "So, you finally bought your own."

"Yes." He, too, looked at the cigarettes. "I mean, no." He made a face, pointing at his forehead. "These are Celia's," he said, suddenly realizing that she knew it, that she was just toying with him, for she picked up the pack and handed it to Celia, then put her own pack on the bar.

"Why don't you admit to yourself who and what you are?" Suzie asked in what he judged to be too critical a tone, a tone Alexie might have employed.

He became aware of his heart beating in his chest and, to calm it, concentrated his gaze on the exquisite straight line of Suzie's nose, deciding to put himself in her hands. "Okay. Who am I?"

"A closeted smoker?" Suzie threw her head back and laughed her wonderful laugh. So, she wasn't annoyed with him, after all.

He shook his head. "Not really. I quit five years ago. I started again today to please you. I mean, as a way to approach you."

"I'm flattered, truly." Her eyes twinkled, and for a moment he saw the child she must have been. "Anyhow, tell me what brought you here. You don't seem the type who keeps late hours."

"Your mental agility," he said. "You're shifting too fast." He tried to smile, and watched as she reached for a bottle behind her and poured from it into his glass.

"What is it?" he asked; the bottle bore no label.

"Good stuff," she said, "courtesy of our friend Nicole. She calls it Satan's Whiskers."

"Satan's Whiskers," Bruno repeated, vaguely recalling having heard or read about it somewhere. "It's a French drink, I think?"

"Right you are." Suzie looked at him with new eyes. "But this here is Nicole's own creative juices. She says it tickles you all the way to heaven. It's a holiday gift, and that's what we're drinking tonight, if it's all right with you."

"Sure." He took a sip, then another. "Kind of bitter. No, sweet."

"Let it grow on you." Suzie took a cigarette from her pack without offering him one. "Drink to your heart's content, everything is on me," she said while filling her own glass.

"Thank you! If I were a woman, I'd be inclined to think you're trying to get me drunk and seduce me."

"I am." Suzie laughed again, and he looked at her, awash in love and gratitude. Here was a woman after his heart, a woman who laughed easily, who smoked and drank, ignoring all the warnings.

"You're very nice to me," he blurted. "I'm not used to women being nice to me. I'm an angry man, you should know that."

"I don't think so," Suzie said. "A bit drunk, maybe, but not angry. You strike me as a very nice man, if a touch too touchy?" She gave him a meaningful look and took a drag on her cigarette. "Overly sensitive, are we?"

As if mesmerized, he followed the smoke coming out of her mouth and rising to the ceiling.

"May I?" He reached for the cigarettes and lit one. "Overly sensitive? Possibly. Women tell me that I'm morose, that I think too much, that I'm too self-absorbed."

"Women are natural complainers, but at least they talk to you." Suzie smiled mischievously. "So, what brings you to our parts?"

"You mean, Snow White or Miami Beach?"

"Both. Are you one of those snowbirds?"

"Snowbird, Snow White." He guffawed, and then, feeling silly, made a gesture with his hand, erasing the comment. "I couldn't fall asleep, and no one was there to massage my earlobes."

The tip of Suzie's tongue appeared between her lips, and the marvel of it resurrected his boyhood fantasy, Miss Lukasic, who appeared before him in her full flesh and blood glory.

"Is that what works for you?" Suzie asked, and it took him a moment to reposition himself in the here and now.

"Worked for my ex-wife," he managed to say casually. "What works for you?"

"Drugs," she said, then smiled. "Kidding, of course. So, what brings you to Miami Beach? You look too young to retire."

Bruno laughed. "Thanks, young is good. I'm a New York refugee. I'm looking for a place to live."

"You don't like New York."

"I do, but I can like it from afar, and when I go back for visits. I used to love my neighborhood, but now it's all restaurants and Whole Foods and Food Emporiums and Fairways, not to mention Zabar's, and people filling their bellies. You may have heard this already, but the worship of food on the Upper West Side is legendary."

"Hmm," Suzie said, disappointing him a little. He had hoped to make her laugh.

"I complain too much," he offered.

"Maybe. Or you're not the same person you were twenty years ago."

"Maybe," he conceded cautiously, and yet he wanted to open his heart to her and tell her everything in direct transmissions from his brain to hers. Tell her everything without ever needing to make sense. Just tell her, tell her, and have her understand. He needed her to listen and comfort him.

"No," he continued. "It has nothing to do with my age. I have to relearn humility. It's easy to become arrogant in the city, the city invites it. It used to be that when you walked down the street, you were likely to catch someone's eye and exchange a friendly smile, but now with everyone busy with one gadget or another, they don't see you. That's why I came here, hoping..."

He looked at her, wanting to catch her eye, but Suzie, a dreamy look on her face, seemed to be elsewhere. He wondered if she was listening to him. "You will laugh, but I often see young women in restaurants or in the park taking out their phones and looking at them fondly, caressing them, maybe cajoling them to make a sound. Maybe it's a new way of bonding. Machines will soon become our true and only companions. I, on the other hand, left my phone behind."

Again he watched Suzie intently, waiting for her to respond, but she took her time, the same dreamy look on her face.

"Machines are our little helpers," she finally said, filling his glass. "Drink and make merry is the only requirement tonight. Here." She raised her glass and clicked it to his. "Drink up!"

Like her, he downed his drink and positioned his glass for a refill. "Your wish is my command," he said, then felt foolish and desperate. He made a face. "I don't think I've ever uttered this line in my life."

At last, Suzie laughed, filling his heart with laughter. "As I said, it's a rebirth. You're emerging from your shell."

He *was* emerging from his shell, how right she was! He focused on her mouth, her lovely mouth. "How come you're sitting on the other side of the bar?"

"I own the place." She offered him a broad smile, and he willingly entered it. If previously he thought she looked noble, like an intelligent thoroughbred, now he thought she looked frisky, mischievous. If on the boardwalk she seemed distant, reserved, she now seemed friendly, direct, challenging. Maybe she was all of those things, an ever-changing seductress.

"So," he said. "You're Snow White."

She looked at him approvingly. "Sometimes."

"And other times?"

"All in good time."

He nodded. "How did you come to own such a business? I mean—" He cut himself short. He didn't like the way he sounded. "I don't know what I mean."

"What's wrong with it?" She cocked her head, mocking him, he thought.

"Nothing is *wrong* with it." He looked away from her. The place, he now noticed, had filled up, and he watched the crowd of mostly middle-aged men laughing and milling around the stage. Watching them, he was suddenly filled with anxiety. No matter how hard he tried, he didn't belong here. He was part of the scene, but he didn't belong. If until that moment he had been oblivious to his surroundings, all at once the place and everything in it seemed coarse and fake to him. He shook his head as if trying to rid himself of something, then rubbed his eyes.

"Are you all right?" Suzie asked, and Celia placed a tall glass of water before him. He drank from it, then dipped his fingers in the glass and dabbed his face and eyes.

"The john's in the back," Suzie said. "If you want to freshen up."

"No, I'm fine." He drank more of the water. "Satan's Whiskers are getting to me. I guess I'm ticklish."

Suzie laughed. "I like you, you know. What's your name, by the way?"

"My name, oh, no." Encouraged by her easy manner, he felt it was now his turn to be whimsical, yet frank and upfront. "You won't like it. Most people don't, but it's Bruno."

"Bruno. I like Bruno, even though you don't look like a Bruno. Italiano?"

"No, Jewish."

"Italian Jew, then."

"We Jews have wandered the earth to atone for our sins. My father was Polish and my mother is half French, so who knows?"

"And your last name?"

"Very German and very boring." He pointed at the bottle. "Am I allowed another drop?"

Suzie poured from the bottle into her and his glass. "Tell me anyway."

Feeling defiant, Bruno sat up straight. "Nope. Not tonight. Maybe tomorrow when you know me a little better?"

Suzie laughed. "All right, dear Bruno, tomorrow. But what if tomorrow never comes?"

"Tomorrow never comes," he repeated slowly, disliking the "dear" she had attached to his name but deciding to ignore it. He concentrated on trying to recall the refrain from *Annie*, but came up with a verse, Matthew 6:34: Do not be anxious about tomorrow, for tomorrow will be anxious for itself. Let the day's own trouble be sufficient for the day.

Smiling, he gazed at his Suzie, feeling calm and at peace. "I don't have kids, as you might have gathered."

Suzie shrugged. "Didn't enter my mind."

He looked at her. "Do you have kids?"

"Nope."

He nodded. "Anyway, I actually liked *Annie*. It felt good to know that millions were watching it with me."

"I know what you mean," Suzie said. "I live alone, too."

Bruno took a moment to digest this piece of information. "That makes two of us. I like living alone, although I don't mind occasional intruders."

"I welcome them!" Again Suzie laughed, and he looked into her mouth, the even row of teeth, the glistening tongue. He loved wide mouths on women. He loved getting lost in them.

"Anyway, you were saying?" Suzie said. "About *Annie*?"

"Oh, yes, I was saying I liked the song, but now it escapes me, something about tomorrow."

"All right, then, we've decided not to worry about tomorrows."

"Worry? Oh, no, I just like to remember things, trivial things. I usually let tomorrow worry about itself." He chuckled, appreciating his small misappropriation, forgetting Suzie, forgetting the bar. He was alone again, a man alone and detached in a strange place far away from home, a man disconnected from all ties, floating in a universe familiar to him. Alone. It was pleasant in that universe. Everything had been suspended, and he was still at the controls.

At his side, Suzie and Celia were talking, and he tried to listen. Celia was talking about a brain, but not the kind that went to college and learned how to do research, how to re-grind the same material over and over only to end up with yet another empty sausage.

"Anyway," Celia was saying, "I told him his emotional life was too crowded for my taste, but the real reason was his open collar Polo shirt. I glimpsed a few white hairs climbing up his throat. A total turnoff."

Bruno listened, mesmerized by her accent, and thankful he wasn't wearing a Polo shirt. "You Brits," he said, his tongue heavy in his mouth, "make English sound so much more delightful than we Americans could ever aspire to."

Suzie and Celia turned to look at him, and then laughed their jolly laughs.

"I'm serious," he continued, suddenly exhausted, "you do."

"You Americans break my heart," Celia said. "We outsiders look at you and you break our heart in your naïve flailing and raving against fate, against the great and vast horizon you have to contend with everywhere you turn. Maybe this has to do with America's position on the planet. I'm not an expert, but the horizon here seems so much vaster than in Europe."

"You're right." Bruno raised his head from the bar. "Was I sleeping?"

"No, just resting," Suzie said. Did she stroke his hair?

"But she is right," he said with an effort, pointing at Celia. "I've noticed the same thing. In Europe, the sky seems more condensed somehow." He paused a moment, wondering if condensed conveyed what he'd meant. "Everything is on a smaller scale. Here the sky is endless, vaster, like Celia says. When is closing time?" He wanted to turn his head, his wonderful and heavy head, to see if other people were still about, but his head wouldn't obey. "I think I'd better turn in," he said.

"We'll take you home soon," Suzie said.

"I don't want to go home," he said, surprised at the new lilt of his voice, the voice of a teenager.

"Of course not." Suzie laughed. Suzie, his little Suzie. His head was spinning, but so what? It was only a head, his head.

He heard himself laugh.

"What's funny?" Suzie asked.

"Nothing, nothing."

Maybe he should go to the john. Someone did say something about the john. I'm not as drunk as all that, he thought. Or maybe he spoke it, for, at last, he heard Suzie's voice again, something about the men's room.

He looked at her, trying to focus and clear the commotion in his eyes.

"The men's room?" he asked, and then remembered that indeed he had wanted to go.

He stood up and waited a moment until he felt sufficiently steady on his feet. Suzie, he noticed, had turned away from him and was speaking to Celia. Well, let them talk, he thought as he began to make his way toward the back. He was quite alert, he thought, even if his vision was a bit blurry. What a life! Who would have thunk! It was long past his bedtime, he was out on the town, talking to his new love, Suzie. How quickly he had found her, and she seemed to like his company.

So, yes, he was still likeable, maybe even loveable. Like a puppy. He wouldn't mind being her puppy. He'd be happy just to be near her, even if only as an amusing accessory.

L'ombre de ton chien. He'd be happy to sing Brel's song to her, to his Suzie. *Ne me quitte pas.* He'd be her puppy or her lover; either/or, he'd be near her. This was certainly a good plan, and a good omen, too. He would start a brand new life and move to Miami Beach, not as a snowbird, but as a permanent resident. He'd have breakfast, lunch, and dinner with Suzie, go for swims in the ocean, get a whole new set of friends and revitalize his spirit, his days and nights. What a plan, what a life.

He reached the back of the bar and walked through an archway that led to a narrow corridor. Supporting himself against the wall, he soon reached a door and a sign that read PRIVATE. He turned the knob, thinking it might be locked, but the door opened and he tiptoed in. Satan's Whiskers, he suddenly remembered and chuckled, wallowing in his drunkenness. He was drinking Satan's Whiskers, and this was Satan's lair, his headquarters. It was a large room, also dimly lit, and surprisingly, instantly inspired a feeling of home, of intimacy. Everything was red—the carpet underfoot, the bedspread, the couch, the armchairs, the lampshades—which suited and pleased him. It soothed the eyes. Soon, he noticed a door at the far end that opened to a bathroom, which he now entered.

Here, too, there was one dominant color: black. The floor, the towels and the bathrobe hanging from a hook on the door, the tile floor.

Maybe Suzie lives here, he thought. Or Celia. On a counter near the sink, he noticed a box of Tampax, a hairbrush, and a few makeup items. Too unsteady on his feet, he sat down on the toilet and tried to concentrate on emptying his bladder, no easy task in his current state. He raised his penis and contemplated the sorry look of his balls, so nice and tight in his youth, now reduced to low-hanging sacs, inspiring pity. Still, when he was erect, their youthful look was restored. At least that.

Finally, mission accomplished, he stood up and went to the bed. Let me just rest here a minute, he thought, slipping off his shoes and crawling onto the bed. Comfy, comfy, he chanted softly as he pulled a pillow from under the bedspread and rested his head.

I am not more guilty than other men, but I have been chosen to see my guilt—he remembered, but couldn't remember where he had heard it, or—was it in a book?

What difference did it make now? When he could finally rest? He couldn't remember much in his state anyway, so let go and rest a while. His brain was not a file cabinet.

My name is Kirsch, Bruno Kirsch, the tape ran in his head. Cherry in German. Used to be Kirschenbaum and now Kirsch. Bruno Kirsch. Heavy of limb and mind at the moment, but still quite vigorous given the need and the right circumstance. Now that I'm resting, where are you, my precious little Suzie? Why not come and lie here next to me? We don't need to touch, or maybe just a little as we cuddle and whisper endearments. Come now, Suzie, you are my longed-for angel. I've ordained your submission, and you are to comply, if only for a few short minutes, blissful for me and hopefully for you. Come lie beside me, Suzie, for it is said:

"If two lie together, then they have heat: but how can one be warm alone?"

Why shy away from one another? Open your arms, we're both made of flesh, and rich blood is coursing in our veins. Come, let me know you, and let you know me…

His head was spinning, so he opened his eyes and struggled to sit up. The sound of drums pounded in his ears. Too drunk, too drunk. How did he allow this to happen?

Well, he was celebrating. It'd been a while since he had any reason or inclination to celebrate. Take them as they come, reach for them when you can, the occasions to celebrate, fleeting as they are. Grab the bull by the horns. It was time to experience the precious miracle of life to the fullest. And he was drinking it now, the cup of life he had been served.

He lay down again. Steady, steady, go slow. He'd rest a bit and then go back to his Suzie, refreshed and clearheaded.

Against you I will fling myself, unvanquished and unyielding, O Death! he recalled. It was good he could still remember lines he had memorized ages ago. Woolf of *The Waves*. The Woolf of his youth when he thought he was in love. In love with the world, in love with Woolf, and with authors like her.

In love! He was watching a movie starring himself and Mary, blessed Mary, whom he had managed to forget, but who now re-asserted herself. Of course, they were arguing about something or other, and this time he ignored her taunts and he kept his mouth shut—a feat!

When arguing with Mary, he tried to hold back the rush of angry words, reciting to himself the Yiddish proverb:

Always make your words sweet; you never know when you'll have to swallow them.

So he knew when to keep his mouth shut, but not so Mary, who loved lecturing him about his many faults. "You never listen to what people actually say. You're focused on your hasty inter-pretation of what they say while preparing your response. You're like a chess player, thinking ahead and planning your attack on your opponent."

"You're not my opponent." He had to admit he appreciated this description of him. Truth be told, he wallowed in it.

"I just can't stand you sometimes," she said.

Silently he observed her, resenting her. He was aware that it was not the Yiddish proverb that made him hold his tongue, but something else, something he had also noted in Rose, a sort of passivity, resignation, when confronted with the unpleasant—not to say rude—behavior of a friend or an acquaintance. He told himself that he, like his mother, was wise keeping his mouth shut, allowing others to rant while he remained calm, observing and listening, taking it all in.

But where was his Suzie? Why didn't she come into the room, looking for him? Maybe the show had begun, and they were all merrily singing while he was lying in bed reliving unpleasant scenes.

He tried to rise, but his muscles wouldn't obey, and he sank back onto the pillow. He was tired, spent. He'd better rest, wait for his Suzie to close up and then drive him to the hotel, or better yet, to her bed. She probably lived not far from his hotel unless she drove to the boardwalk to take her morning walk.

But how could she rise so early if she worked so late?

Indistinct shapes danced behind his trembling eyelids, and he laughed or wanted to laugh. Maybe he just smiled since no sound issued from him. Smiling was good enough. It relaxed your facial expression and brought light into your soul, soothing your feverish brain. Let Mary come in and wake him with a kiss.

No, not Mary, Suzie. Let her come in and kiss him and make him eighteen again, make him aware of how barren his life had been before she stepped into it, into him. Let her come into his arms, let them lie together and cuddle, let him rest his head and sigh with relief.

What a full and rich day he was having! Was it possible that only this morning Mary had left? And his trip to Aventura, and the old lady and her ice cream. No, no, that happened yesterday. This morning he'd had breakfast at the café and Suzie, his Suzie, arrived. And the pool and the obese kids, and the movies he watched, and the drunk Russians asking for ice. And the two queens he saw on the way, the stars of the show taking place on the stage at this very minute, and he was missing it all.

No great loss. What he can't see today, he'll see tomorrow. There's always tomorrow, even if tomorrow never comes, even if it only comes for some but not for others.

It was all so strange, the days of todays and the days of tomorrows. How muddled everything becomes when you let a Suzie pour Satan's Whiskers into your glass. You don't even know Suzie. She could be a trapdoor to hell or to heaven. He was risking life and he was risking death, why not, what else was there to risk?

Interesting how he came to be the person he was. Too often misunderstood, his attempts to communicate falling short. Only Rose, yes, only Rose knew and understood him, but when she looked at him, he thought he could sense she was looking at him in a way that told him she understood far more than he knew. She saw something he couldn't see, something she would not tell him, maybe because she wished to spare his feelings, maybe because she knew it would do no good to tell him because whatever she saw was so much the core of him, there was no point in commenting on it and advising him to change.

Maybe he was blind, a lacking human being, but not more so than others. In one way or another, we are all blind, he told his students. We are misguided walking shells, reservoirs of useless information. Knowledge, real knowledge, comes from within. If you try hard and access such knowledge, count yourself lucky. It's a rare gift.

As he spoke the words, he would suddenly realize that he had raised his voice and let his arms become implements of passion and persuasion. He probably seemed absurd to these young kids facing an open road of clear goals while a ranting, misguided professor tried to block their view. What did they care about rare gifts? They needed to pass the exams and get good grades, and hopefully get laid at the end of the day. Scoring on all levels was the thing. His sermons about knowledge probably didn't reach them, but he hoped one day when they were ripe for it, they would hear his voice again rising in their memory and they would get that he spoke to them from deep in his heart.

Was he awake? Asleep? He thought he heard movement. He thought he heard someone whisper his name, but he was elsewhere. He couldn't be bothered. There was only so much he could absorb all at once. People crowding over him, around him, pushing, wanting this, wanting that, always demanding. Please stay away and leave me alone, all of you. I've had my share of the good, and I've had my share of the bad. Now I need to rest, rest and restore.

How words comforted him. Rest and restore, how simple! He should have told his students "Rest and restore!" But it was too late now, as he would never stand in front of a class again. He would go to Akumal, his private paradise, where he would rest and restore in peace and quiet.

Bruno laughed with sudden joy. He laughed in his head, he laughed in the vacuum of his dream—it wasn't so bad, after all. Yes, like all living things, his day would come and time would end.

He would be dead to others, but hopefully not to himself. Maybe life did have another dimension, another form where time counted for nothing. Where rushing from here to there, the heart always pounding with anticipation and panic would cease. If indeed we were cursed by the Almighty in the Garden of Eden, what was the point of the entire exercise, the entire enterprise? God should have called it quits right there and then. Why go on if we are doomed? Why go on if *in sorrow shalt thou eat of it all the days of thy life?*

"Oh, Bruno, Bruno, where art thou?" someone called from somewhere, accelerating his heartbeat. He was right here. Why was that someone shouting? He was right here at the crossroad. What was one to do? Continue on or stand a while and contemplate the signpost? Maybe the signpost was right, suggesting it was time he took a good look at himself. But maybe he, too, was right when he told the signpost he was who he was.

On the whole, he was a good man, and reasonable too. What did they all want from him? Why did he have to put up with people's never-ending and often perplexing demands? And why was it he who had to obey Mary and embrace her ways and habits and not the other way around? Who was she to claim power and control over him? And when would he finally stop explaining and defending himself in his head? No peace and quiet for the weary until it was time for the grave. In the cosmic scheme of things, what was the point of all this fruitless agitation? Can he get lost in his own mind and never find his way back?

The party! Is it still going on?

He rose from the bed and walked out to join them in the large room. It was dimmer than before, and people were seated at a few scattered tables facing the stage where a performance was in progress. So he missed some of it, but he could still catch the rest of it.

Some kind of music—African?—blasted from the speakers, the bass pounding in his heart, spreading in wide circles. A woman, sitting on a tall stool on the stage, was unbuttoning her shirt, and then let it drop to the floor. She undid her bra, and her large breasts floated into view, bouncing with new freedom.

Bruno giggled—this was too funny! He wanted to laugh but was mindful of the others and of the solemnity of the moment. A woman revealing her breasts was still a sacred occasion. Comic but sacred.

Men are such fools! Bruno laughed soundlessly. Why interfere with the pleasure of others? Let them eat up those heavy breasts. And why is she hiding her face? Maybe she's embarrassed, just a member of the audience and not a professional stripper.

So no more lip-synching and Christmas carols, just a cheap performance by an amateur.

People everywhere. A curse and a blessing. Not on bread alone, etc.

He glanced around the room, hoping to spot Suzie or Celia, but they were nowhere in sight. This is odd, he thought, then panicked. He was all alone in a place where he knew no one, and no one knew him. Was he safe among these strangers? He must keep his cool. No one in the room even looked in his direction, no one seemed to have noticed him. Suzie and Celia were probably some-where in the back, preparing to close down for the night. He might as well join the others. Find a nice table and enjoy himself like the rest of them.

"Is there room for me at the table?" he called out in too loud a voice, which momentarily confused him. Why was he shouting? What was he thinking?

"What table, Bruno?" he heard a voice ask.

"A table," he repeated stubbornly. His head hurt. Maybe he needed an aspirin.

"What table, Bruno?" There went the voice again.

"I don't know." Was he taking an exam? Suddenly he saw it. "Maybe the Passover table, when Alexie threw a vase at me?"

"Why did she throw a vase at you?"

"I think I must have offended her, something to do with an entry ticket? She's always been such a snob, always carrying on, superior-like."

"But she's your sister, Bruno. She's family."

"Yes, I know, but my father had died, and it was just the three of us at the table. Alexie and I exchanged some words, Alexie boasting to Rose that she would only date guys who were well-read, and I, trying to imagine the kind of men who would date my sister and feeling sorry for them, said something about books be-ing the entry ticket to her saintly vagina or something like that."

"And she threw a vase at you?"

"She did, yes she did, but not right away. First she screamed at me, telling me to mind my own business, and then, I think I said she should be careful, that her I.Q. plunged when she screamed."

"That was naughty of you," Suzie chided, and Bruno smiled and lowered his head.

"Yes, Suzie. It was naughty of me, but it felt good."

"Naughty always feels good, yes?"

"I imagine it does. Anyway, what are you doing on stage? I think it's kind of grotesque, you exposing yourself like that."

"Why grotesque? How about generous?"

"I don't know, you're the owner. It doesn't look right, it doesn't fit."

"Don't be silly, Bruno. We're among friends, we share."

"Yeah, yeah, I've heard it all before." He needed to rest. He sank his head onto his chest, and then looked up again. Suzie had put on a robe and joined him at the table. He looked at her, expecting to see a new line of vulgarity in her face, like Cain's mark, but she seemed as beautiful and pure as before.

"Where are your crutches?" he asked, suddenly remembering she seemed free of them onstage.

"Right here, Bruno, why?"

He looked under the table and saw her crutches lying at her side, one on top of the other. "Why did you do it, Suzie? I know it's none of my business, but why would a woman like you do a thing like that?"

Suzie laughed. "A woman like me, that's a good one." She slapped her thigh. "The queens asked me to."

"What queens?"

"These queens." Suzie pointed at the two women he had seen on the street.

"What kind of queens are they?" he asked and Suzie's laugh rang out again. It was good to hear her laugh.

"You can't be so out of it!"

"I'm not out of it, I'm in it," he protested, then recalled he was speaking with Suzie, not Mary. "Well, I'm not totally out of it, just a bit slow at times. I can't find my place."

"Are we feeling terribly sorry for ourselves?"

"Whatever you say, Suzie. It's been a long and tiring day."

"Why don't you lie down for a bit?"

"Yes, I think I will." A thought slid into his head. "We're like husband and wife, my Suzie. You're the good wife, advising me to lie down when I'm tired."

"Yes, that's a good way to look at it," Suzie said, and he rose and went to the bed.

Suzie followed him. "I think you'd better take off your clothes and get under the covers, you'll be more comfortable. Here, let me help you."

He lay down on the bed, and she helped him, pulling down his pants, and he vaguely sensed she was standing upright without the use of her crutches.

"Why didn't you speak to me when you saw me on the boardwalk?" he recalled. "I thought you didn't like me. I tried to get your attention, but you ignored me."

Suzie tucked him in, hovering above him and smiling like the angel she was. "I don't know why. Maybe I was waiting for some-thing?"

"For what?"

"I don't know. The fact is we found one another."

"Yes, we did," he said, and a blissful calm descended on him.

He heard Suzie laugh. "Why didn't *you* talk to me when you saw me on the boardwalk?"

"Me?" He was glad for the question. It meant she had ex-pected something from him. "I thought you looked severe, not easy to approach. I thought you probably found me old and un-attractive. In fact, what did you think of me when you first saw me on the boardwalk?"

She didn't answer right away, so he opened his eyes and sought her in the dark. "Where are you, Suzie?" he called, sitting up.

"Right here, Bruno, near the window, smoking a cigarette."

"Oh, good." He fell back onto the pillow. "I bet you thought, *there goes a good-looking man with a small belly.*"

Suzie laughed again, delighting him. "No, not good-looking. Pleasant-looking is more like it."

"Pleasant?" He was surprised.

"Yes. I liked the tranquility I saw in your face."

Tranquility! "What else?"

She came back to the bed. "You seemed lonely. Maybe needy?"

"Needy, huh?" He sighed. "All things considered, I've had my share of the good and the bad. I really shouldn't complain. Do we have windows in here?"

"Yes, of course. Why do you ask?"

"I don't know, just something that popped into my head."

"I have to go out for a moment. Try to rest, okay? Can you do that for me? I'll be right back."

He turned onto his side and pulled the cover over his head. It had taken a while, but now he was finally feeling good, complete somehow. He and Rose were visiting her sister Molly in the psychiatric ward. It was awful, the obscenities she hurled at them, and Rose weeping, and he, numb with worry for Molly, for Rose, pulled Rose away.

"Why did they bind her to the bed?" Rose had asked

"Because they had to," he told her.

And then he remembered he was missing the performance, he was missing all the fun, and where was his Suzie? Why hadn't she come? He threw off the covers and made his way back to the large room. He heard laughter all around, which pleased and displeased him. They were having a good time, and all of it without him. Why didn't she come to get him? He was still alive, he was still part of the scene, why not include him? And now more laughter from invisible corners, and his Suzie is nowhere in sight.

And then, without him being prepared or suspecting anything, strong arms seized him—Why? What have I done?

"Quiet, Bruno," someone whispered, and, in his stupor, he realized it was Celia.

"Celia, where's Suzie? What have I done? What are you doing?"

"You're naked, Bruno. We have to put you in bed, don't fight us."

Naked? "What are you talking about?" He heard himself shout. "I was never naked, not like you mean."

More laughter. How annoying they all are, having their fun with him. His dignity is at stake, he must defend himself. "You're all a bunch of scoundrels, you can't fool me."

"No one is here to fool you, Bruno. You were naked when you came out of your mother's womb, remember?"

"Well, yes," he whimpered. Indeed, he *is* naked. How did this happen? Thankfully, here is Suzie and a tall shadow next to her. They are tucking him in, whispering.

"It's raining hysterically," Suzie said to the tall shadow. "Tie him to the bed."

"Where did you find this loser?" said the shadow, and Suzie laughed. "Believe it or not, he showed up on my doorstep."

"Suzie, don't talk about me this way, it's not fair," he wanted to say but couldn't open his mouth.

"Should we cover his face?" the shadow asked, filling his heart with terror.

But soon Suzie's calm voice said, "No, no need for that."

"You're right, Suzie," he said, greatly relieved. "You don't need to bind me to the bed. I'm fine, I promise you."

"It's just a precaution, Bruno. You needn't worry. Remember Samson and Prometheus?"

"Yes, of course." But he also remembered Delilah and Pandora, and *Mingle together all things loveliest, sweetest, and best, but look that you also mingle therewith the opposites of each.* How automatic the brain! "What did you put in my glass?" he asked, trying not to sound querulous or suspicious.

"You mean other than liquor?"

"Satan's Whiskers, remember?"

Suzie laid a soothing palm on his forehead. "I think it's the cigarettes, Bruno. You've smoked a lot tonight, and you're not accustomed to the poison anymore."

"Oh, the poison, yes. I need to put my trust in someone. I need to trust someone." He reached for her, pleading. "You understand what I mean? Don't you, Suzie?"

"Of course I do. All is well, Bruno, one must have trust in order to live. Now, just lie down and try to rest. I'm right here beside you."

"Yes, right here beside me." *Thank goodness*, he thought, determined to resume his rest and restore.

Rest and restore—a must!

But soon, his feverish mind piped up. "Suzie, you too devour men?"

"Why yes, of course. We all do, and Tonio is here. You remember Tonio?"

"Tonio? Who is Tonio?"

"He served your dinner last night. He likes you. He wants to devour you."

"You're too funny!" Bruno heard himself howl with delight. "You make me feel like a boy."

"No, I'm not being funny, it's true. Tonio likes you. Do you like Tonio?"

"I like him all right."

"Do you mind if he joins you in bed?"

"I don't know what you mean." Bruno tried to laugh, but then, right next to him, someone indeed was getting into the bed. "No," he wanted to shout, but his cry died in the air. This is getting out of hand, he thought. This must stop. "Suzie," he called. "Suzie!"

"This is how women feel when they're violated," someone whispered in his ear.

"It's not my business, why do you bother me? I've never violated a woman in my life. Suzie? Where are you? Suzie?!"

"I'm here, Bruno. Relax. Try to sleep, you're exhausted."

"Yes, I am. Who's in bed with me?"

"No one, Bruno. Sleep. You're tired. You need to rest."

"I want to go on a trip."

"You will, but first you need to rest."

"Rest and restore!"

How quiet it is! Again, they left him behind and went back to the party. Well, who cares? He can rest now, undisturbed.

Ah, blessed pillows! Indeed, he's had it easy, maybe too easy. He's never been tested, he never fought in a war, he never went hungry, never hankered after a piece of bread like his father in the camps, his father who had told him and Alexie they would never know the true meaning of hunger. All the rest was noise, his father had said.

Indeed, Bruno thought. It was all noise. A new class of idiots materialized every day, a new set of chattering monkey-experts filling our heads with babble. The tower of Babel rose before him, the tower of human hubris, the tower of self-interest and arrogance. How long can man sustain himself on spiritual emptiness and chaos? One was better off living quietly, free of ambition, following his own advice, his own voice.

Someone, maybe the shadow, whispered in his ear. "Why are you so cautious and stingy about life and pleasure? Want to live forever?"

"Yes, I do," he muttered. "What's it to you?"

"I didn't mean to criticize, Bruno. No need to get upset, you know?" Suzie leaned forward so he could see her face.

"Well," he said. "Why argue? Everything under the sun dies. I'm not special."

"Is this King Solomon speaking?"

King Solomon? What did King Solomon have to do with him lying here on this bed? "No, it's me speaking. There are no kings here as far as I can tell."

Suzie laughed. "But you're wrong, Bruno, see? You're special to me, that's what I meant."

She was too sweet—what was her game? What made her think he belonged to her to do with as she pleased? He'd better keep his guard up until he figured out what she and the others were up to. It was no accident he ended up on this bed. She must have planned it. People were mean, too often for no reason at all, just to pass the time. They talked about you behind your back, usually nonsense they may have heard in passing from someone else and, without verifying or stopping to think if it made sense, they spread and perpetuated malice, filling the universe with endless, harmful chatter.

Quiet please, I want quiet, he thought he'd heard himself shout and instinctively pressed his hand to his mouth. He'd better keep quiet, or they'll lock him up.

What a life! We chatter like monkeys and then we chatter no more.

He must have fallen asleep or dozed for a while, for the image of Aschenbach slumped in a beach chair, appeared before him.

Oh, Aschenbach, Aschenbach. Poor, poor Aschenbach. In your rumpled silk suit and your good Prussian manners. In the end, they didn't prove very useful, did they? Your education and academic credentials failed you as well.

How many circles in Hell? he wondered. He had probably gone through limbo, most of his life he had spent in limbo. He had probably gone through lust and gluttony and maybe greed and wrath and heresy but no violence, fraud, or treason, and was now ready to exit and enter purgatory. A Jew, was he even allowed entry? And why fill his head with nonsense? He was much better off ascending the ladder of *sefirot* toward a deeper consciousness of God. He must always remember where he came from.

"Suzie, are you here?"

"Yes, Bruno, I'm right here at your side."

"If only I could tell you my thoughts, but it's all a jumble. You're so good to me. You're my swan song, Suzie. I'm off to see my maker."

Suzie laughed softly. "No, you're not. It's too early. You've got a good many years left in you. Chin up! You're still in good shape."

He was pleased. So it wasn't time yet. Many good years were still buried in him. "You know, I almost came here last night to look for you. Tonio sent me, but I went home instead."

"Yes, I know, he told me. He comes here often after his shift ends."

"He put his hand on my shoulder, which I thought was highly unusual."

"Well, Bruno, maybe in New York and other artificial cities it's unusual, but not around here. And he is not your usual waiter. He's an artist. Everything he does comes from the source. He's a friendly guy, our Tonio." She laughed her charming laugh which, briefly, made him uncomfortable, for he could not be sure what was so funny about Tonio being friendly.

"I thought he assumed I was gay."

"Are you?"

"At the moment, yes, I'm very gay." Now he laughed, and his Suzie took a deep breath. "Is that what you mean by wanting to devour me?"

"Yeah, kind of," she said.

"Every night before falling asleep, I ask myself: Did I do something important and worthwhile today?"

"And your answer?"

"Depends. Lately the answer has been no rather than yes."

"That's okay, Bruno. That's why you came here. You needed to take a break."

"Suzie, will I go back to normal later?"

"Later? You're normal now."

Normal now. Maybe his Suzie was right.

"You know me better than I know myself." He shut his eyes, willing himself to fall asleep. You ran away from death, and death followed you. How did that story go? A story his father liked to tell, about a Hasid who escapes to a nearby town to avoid the angel of death, only to encounter him there and to learn that this town, where he had sought refuge, had been in the plan all along.

Suzie, his angel-confessor, his sweet angel on earth.

"I had big dreams, Suzie. I wanted a big life for myself. Your usual American fame and riches, if only to prove something. It was very selfish of me, I know, but look where I ended up."

"But you're wrong, Bruno. You're having a big life right now. Here in this room with me."

Yes! This was something he could believe. Now he felt alert and on the go. "Help me here, Suzie. Do we have true and reliable premonitions of death or is it simply our everyday fear?"

"I can't say, Bruno."

"At any rate, I'm not ready to go. I need to write my father's story."

"Is it a good story, Bruno?"

How soothing to hear her say his name. "Yes, Suzie, I believe it is. I want to do it for Rose."

"Of course, Bruno. You're a good son, always have been."

"Are you Jewish, Suzie?"

Suzie laughed. "No, Bruno, I'm not. Does it matter?"

"No, it doesn't matter. My Mary isn't Jewish either. She loves mirrors, did I tell you? She has many mirrors of varying sizes in every room in her apartment. Every time she goes past one, she glances at her image and adjusts her expression to fit her idea of herself as a still attractive and desired woman. She does this openly, without trying to hide her vanity, and this, I have to admit, endeared her to me."

"Mary? Your wife?"

"No, my wife was Ellen, and she was Jewish. You and Mary may meet in Heaven, but I, the cursed Jew, will never make it to your Heaven. We Jews have our own spa."

"You're funny, little Bruno." Suzie stroked his arm. "Maybe there's a connecting corridor and conjugal visits are allowed?"

"No way in hell!" Bruno heard himself laugh.

Someone was crying in the corner, alarming him. "Suzie? I'm so sorry. Suzie? Please? I didn't mean to offend you. Do you forgive me?"

But Suzie gave no reply, and he felt his insides turn in shame and fear. "Who's there?" he shouted. "Why are you crying?"

"It's me, Bruno, Rose."

"Mother?" His heart sank. For her to see him like this! "How did you get here? Why are you crying?" He tried to sit up, but he was too weak. He heard Rose sniffle, and yet she wouldn't respond.

"Rose, please, you must talk to me. I'm your son, you must answer."

"You're dying, my son, and it's painful. It pains me to watch it."

"It's preordained, Mother. You know how these things go."

"Yes, I know. The same happened with your father. How my voice echoes in here! This is too strange, to bury him, and now you, and you so young still and full of life. It breaks my heart."

He listened to her sob, and he rolled from side to side, as if wishing to smother her pain and his. He didn't want her to suffer. This wasn't in the plan, it all went so wrong on him.

"Where's Alexie? Why isn't she here? She will comfort you."

Rose sighed. "You know how busy she is."

"Yes, I know." He ventured cautiously. "Are you disappointed in me? Your only son?"

"No, Bruno, you've always been very dear and special to me."

"I always felt I could have done a little better."

"It's not always up to us, Bruno. You did your best, and that's all we can do."

"Yes, that's true," he said, suddenly overwhelmed. Something switched or shifted in his brain. "At least I tried. Remember the *siddur* father gave me? I can still recite from it."

He shut his eyes. Yes, he could still recite from it. Already at the young age of thirteen, he felt he was learning more from the *siddur* than from his textbooks. All that he read in the *siddur* felt right, so old and wise. A person's speech conveys the person, good or bad, revealing the soul of the speaker. A pure soul is not capable of uttering falsehoods and foul language. Speaking ill of others and idle gossip are like an arrow shot in the dark, an arrow that will turn around and strike the heart of the speaker. A boomerang! Stay away from anger, pride and flattery, avoid lies and deceit. Remember three things and you'll keep from trouble: Whence you came, where you're going, and who you'll have to report to. You came from a putrid drop, you'll be buried in the ground and will report to God, the King of Kings, the Divine. Love God with all thy heart.

God is his witness, he did try mightily to follow these guidelines, not always successfully, but at least he tried. He was always aware of his shortcomings and, like the *siddur* says, he was not at peace with himself.

Tears rolled down his cheeks. Who will say Kaddish for him? Maybe Jonathan, Alexie's oldest. Why wasn't his family gathered around him, as was customary?

"You were always a stubborn child, Bruno, you questioned everything. The order of things irritated you because you didn't understand it. Even the order of the alphabet irritated you. You couldn't understand why A came first and not third, for instance. You accepted numbers, though. One was one, and two was two."

"I must have been a burden to you and Dad."

"No, Bruno, we loved you and we still love you."

"I remember something you told me when I was little. You said to me: 'Do you know what life is? Life is doing good, helping an old lady carry her groceries, helping a blind man cross the street.'"

"Yes, this is a good lesson to remember."

Ah, blessed love. Blessed memory. How deeply he felt it now, the true meaning of it. He'd come all this way to realize something he'd known all along. Yes, all along and ever since time began for him. Through all the struggles he endured. Through all the hurdles placed in his path for reasons he couldn't fathom. And now, finally, he'd be going back to the beginning. To the source. How mysterious, and yet how simple. Something he'd known all along but was too busy or lazy to focus on.

"I only regret disappointing you. I never allowed myself to be goofy and passionate, spontaneous. I was always cautious, too cautious, I think. But—" He chuckled. "It's too late for acrimony. I'll say hello to Father for you. And for Alexie."

"Good, Bruno, good."

"I never told Alexie this, but I'm grateful she gave you grandkids. After all is said and done, I think you've done a swell job raising me the way you did. I wouldn't be here if it weren't for you and dad, and I don't just mean the physical fact of giving life to me. You were the best parents a child could have."

Again, tears filled his eyes. Sentimental tears that come from joy, from a cleansed heart. A heart ready for an audience with the King of Kings. For it is said: *First they should ask the whereabouts of the King's house, and then they should ask where the King is!*

"And I'll say hello to Aschenbach, too!"

"Who's Aschenbach?"

"A friend."

He was shivering. Did he have a cold? If he did, it was getting worse. His throat hurt, and his nose was stuffy. He wasn't the type to rush to a doctor or hospital. Still, he could get a heart attack and no one would be there to help him. He would die here on this bed and wouldn't be discovered until morning when the maids arrived with their cheerful Spanish voices and found him, already cold and stiff. His own beloved body, his very dear flesh and blood, with the moles he inherited from Rose and the hockey scar he bore on his forehead as a badge of honor.

"Remember, Rose, when I was little and was rushed to the hospital, and you cried while the nurses held me down so they could inject me and bring the fever down?"

"Rose isn't here, Bruno, it's me, Suzie."

Ah, Suzie! So he wasn't in his hotel room, after all. He was here with Suzie, in her wild and sleazy Snow White.

"Oh, Suzie, my savior!"

Suzie laughed, or so he imagined. At any rate, what he heard was pleasing to the ear.

"When I think about you, it's usually in the negative," Mary said. "You don't like this, you don't approve of that. And the list is long, Bruno. When you die, you will die alone."

He smiled. We all die alone, he wanted to say, but he knew what she meant. "But you'll be there," he said affably.

"Don't count on it," she snorted.

Well, you can't win them all. He had what he had, and he didn't have what he didn't have.

"Go deep into your heart, Bruno. That's where salvation waits."

"Suzie, is that you?"

"Yes. Go deep into your heart. Go now, Bruno."

"I will. Deep into my heart. Tell Mary to go away. She is bad news. She makes me feel ugly. We always made each other feel ugly."

"She is gone, Bruno. Don't pay her any mind. Do you love Jesus?"

Jesus? "Of course I love Jesus. I love all Jews, at least in the abstract. And I don't believe he said all the things they say he said, like turn the other cheek, or that he who loves his father and mother more than he loves Jesus is not worthy of Jesus. A Jew would never dream up such a thing—parents always come first for a Jew. It's one of the Ten Commandments. Memorize the Fifth Commandment: *Honor thy father and thy mother: that thy days may be long upon the land.*

"Remember that Jesus, first and foremost, was a Jew, an *illui*, some say, a prodigy, in the study of the Torah. If he had known that countless Jews and others would be massacred in his name, he would have kept his message to himself."

"It's hard to keep a message to oneself. We need to voice it."

"True, but it was never his intention to launch a new religion, he said so himself. It's the P.R. and marketing people who took over as they always do, inventing holy ghosts and messiahs, vilifying the old and glorifying the new. Imagine the mess if a messianic age were to arrive, and a loving God would not only do away with death, but would retroactively resurrect the dead. Imagine the billions of resurrected souls attempting to locate their loved ones. Lists upon lists would be drawn and published in the daily newspapers. Special institutions would be erected to deal with the problem, not very different from the confusion after the Holocaust when family members sought each other. Thank Jesus for the internet!"

Suzie laughed. "Amen!"

Amen, indeed. "It's a Hebrew word, you know."

"No, I didn't. Is it important?"

"I don't know. Maybe. I bet many Christians don't know this. For many centuries they didn't know or wouldn't acknowledge their Lord and Savior was a Jew."

"That's old history, Bruno. Don't trouble your head over it."

"Well." Bruno sighed. Indeed, why trouble his head?

"Are you sad?" Suzie asked, and he thought he heard concern in her voice. She did care, and this, for now, eased his heart.

"I'm exhausted, Suzie, outpouring myself to you. Soon, there'll be nothing left. Maybe just a small puddle, like in scary movies."

"There's still plenty of you left, Bruno. No need for you to worry."

"Oh, Suzie, with you at my side, I have no worries. You know, I lived alone most of my life. When you live alone, as soon as you wake up, you're confronted with the vacuum of your days. No one is there on the pillow next to you to reassure you otherwise. On the other side of it, if the head on the pillow is intolerable, then you're in for another kind of hell. I felt feverish before, but I feel much better now."

"You've had a rough week with Mary. She wounded you, and now you need to recuperate."

"True. You're my angel and my good nurse." He heard a whisper, and he tensed up. "What did you say?"

"I said I was your good everything," Suzie said in a loud voice, if a bit too loud.

"Yes, of course." He took a moment to think about loving the good nurse. "Maybe I love you more than I can bear to admit, huh? I borrowed this line from a silly movie. I hope you don't mind. It feels good to say it."

Suzie or someone else whispered in his ear, "Words have consequences, Bruno. There are more pets in America than people."

"I never had one," he admitted sorrowfully, remembering the black cat he saw at the bus stop to Aventura.

"It's not too late, you can still get one."

"You think so?"

"You have to make plans. You must keep in touch."

"Yes, you're right," he said, then thought better of it. "Why are you telling me this?"

"Telling you what?"

"About plans, about pets." He saw himself as a snail, creeping on its stomach, its antennae on the move. "Oh, Suzie," he called, "my brain is on fire." A wide field opened before him—life was given to us *gratis* so why the bickering? Why did he feel that he had been left behind? That something was missing?

A phrase played in his head: *Oh, what is man, that he can grumble about himself!*

"True," he heard Suzie say.

"What?"

"What you just said."

"I spoke it? I thought I only thought it."

"You said it."

"Funny!"

This may turn out to be the most beautiful night of his life! He got to say all he'd always wanted to say, but never found a good listener.

He began to laugh softly, then felt his body convulsing with laughter. He placed a hand on his chest, as if to stop his heart from leaping out. "Through me, you pass into the city of woe," he recited, then waited for Suzie to respond, but she offered no comment or indication that she had heard him. No matter. He felt comfortable with Suzie, even when she said nothing. The mere fact of her presence was enough.

"Are you okay?"

"Sure I'm okay," he said. "I'm just laughing."

"You are?"

"Of course, why shouldn't I?"

"Why are you laughing?"

"Nothing in particular. I'm just…. Well, happy! I feel happy."

"Good, I'm glad."

He didn't appreciate her sardonic tone, but he was not going to let such a small thing bother him, not now. At long last he was feeling good, happy, so happy he wanted to sing. How long had it been since he felt such *joy?*

He stretched his facial muscles. His eyes were open, and he felt his radiance spreading its goodness all around him.

"Do you remember?" he asked. "I forget who said it, something about old songs. Old songs are more than just tunes, they're small houses where our hearts once lived. Does it ring a bell?"

"No, but it's a nice idea."

It was more than a nice idea, he thought. A small house where your heart once lived. He tried to find her, even turned his head in the direction of her voice, but he couldn't see her. "Where are you?"

"Right here, Bruno."

Bruno. Yes. His name was Bruno—a name he'd hated as a child, a name he had inherited from a grandfather he never knew. A grandfather who had perished in a Nazi death camp. Oh, those Nazis, how much he loathed them throughout his childhood. "A child's hate is pure. Did you know that, Suzie?"

"Yes, Bruno. Everything that comes from a child is pure."

"True. I was a cute little boy myself, I think I already told you." He allowed himself to drift, as if browsing through a photo album, and he came upon the flushed and exultant face of a young boy dancing the *hora* on Simchat Torah.

Yes, he recognized the face. It belonged to him when he was ten or eleven, a young idealistic boy, his entire life a promise stretching before him.

"You're still very cute, my dear."

"Thanks." Again, the generic "my dear" grated at him. "What did you put in my drink?" he asked, lightly, not caring really, just curious.

"Nothing. I think it's you, not the drink."

"What is me?"

"I don't know." He heard her laugh. "Do you know?"

"So you're laughing now."

"That's because you're funny, you make me laugh."

"I thought you were laughing at me, the idiot."

"No, I would never laugh at you."

He breathed a sigh of relief. "Thanks for telling me this, Suzie. I like to hear you laugh. You have a beautiful laugh, that's the first thing that attracted me to you. And, of course, your name."

"You like my name?"

"I do, I do. Like a marriage vow… imagine!"

He found himself in a deep cave, then emerged in a whisper. "When I was a very young boy, I used to sit and watch my father. He always had a toothpick in his mouth. I hated that toothpick and so did my mother. We were both worried that one day he would swallow it, but, thankfully, he never did."

"Was he a smoker trying to quit?"

"No, just a smoker. Sometimes he'd have them both in his mouth, the toothpick and the cigarette. He had many secrets, not the usual kind of secrets, but painful secrets."

"He was a sad man," Suzie said.

Sad was not the word, but what other words were available to them? To those who survived? He recalled reading about a group of survivors who couldn't live indoors after the war. They became wanderers, rejecting a culture that bred *petit-bourgeois* ideals hand in hand with mass murderers.

It was strange how he went from here to there. A nomad's life would suit him best, but was it achievable for someone like him? And where was the real Bruno hiding? Would Suzie bother to look for him?

"Suzie, I'm sweating like a pig. Do you have a towel I can use?"

"Of course, Bruno, here, let me wipe your sweat."

"You're my ministering angel."

"But you don't believe in angels."

He nodded his heavy head. "You're right, I don't. Or I never used to. Still, it's never too late to believe. I need to empty myself. I want to feel light again."

She laughed. "Like in the womb?"

The womb? "What do you mean?" he asked, trying to suppress the sudden wave of hostility toward her. "Why the womb?" He looked in the direction of the voice and thought he glimpsed her face as a white stain in the dark.

"Why not? It's a place like any other."

"You mean death, don't you?" As he said this, once again he lost her face. He felt irritated and confused. What were they talking about? What did she put in his drink? Was he having a good time? "I lost your face," he complained.

"It's not lost," she whispered back, "it's elsewhere."

"Elsewhere where? Are you a sorceress?"

Again she laughed, and this time her laugh comforted him. He smiled. "I'm a magician, too. Ellen used to say I have the magic touch."

"Did she?"

"I used to massage her earlobes. Did I tell you about Ellen?"

"Your ex-wife?"

"That's right, my ex-wife. What a life. It's so good to laugh once in a while. I feel liberated." He didn't actually hear himself laugh, but his chest heaved with laughter.

"I'm your nurse," Suzie said. "Your appointed nurse."

"Taradiddle, taradiddle." Bruno impatiently waved his hand, erasing the nonsense of her words. "I don't need a nurse. Who appointed you?"

"Quiet, Bruno, you need to rest."

He became agitated. What nerve! "Why did you say you were my nurse? What's wrong with me? Why do I need a nurse?"

"I didn't say you needed a nurse, I said you needed to rest."

"Did you call a doctor?"

"No. Do you want me to call one?"

"Not yet." He gave it some thought. "Unless you think it's necessary. You can't expect me to be a good judge of my condition, not at the present moment anyway."

"It won't be easy today. It's Christmas, you know, but I could take you to the hospital."

"Hospital!" Bruno wailed. "Why, Suzie? Why do you want to send me off to a hospital?"

"We're not sending you off to a hospital. It's just an option to consider."

"An option to consider?" He raised his hands to his face and wiped his sweat. "But why? I don't think I want to go to some hospital and lie on a bed in a hallway."

"We have modern facilities here, but if you don't want to go, we won't."

"Unless…." Maybe she knew best, maybe he should let her decide. "Unless you think we should? What's wrong with me? Am I sick?"

"Not at all, Bruno, you're in good hands."

"Are you sure? What is it you put in my drink?"

"Are you hungry?"

"No," he said belligerently, then watched with amazement as she rose from the chair and walked away from him easily without her crutches. "I thought you only had one leg."

"Really? Why?"

"Why?! Because! You had crutches. Where are your crutches?"

"Right here." She raised both hands, and the crutches stuck out toward him in two parallel lines.

"Oh," he said, mollified.

"Happy?"

"Yes." He smiled like a child proven wrong by a kind adult. "I do feel a bit feverish," he whispered. "Could it be the flu?"

"No, Bruno, I don't think so."

She sounded so wise and responsible, he felt he must trust her. She knew and understood him. He should be grateful.

"I live in a strange universe," he confessed.

"What's so strange about it?"

"Everything. Plants, people. My own thoughts are a mystery to me."

"Yes, thoughts sometimes do take us to strange places."

"And you can't discuss this kind of thing with people, with close friends, or even a shrink. The truth is, they're just as lost and confused and worried as you are."

"You're right, my dear Bruno. If you carry an argument or a thought far enough, things do begin to look and sound strange."

"What do you mean?" *That "dear" again.*

"Maybe thinking too much and dwelling on things is not good for you. Maybe you should try some other kind of exercise."

"You mean, run away from my thoughts?"

"Yes, something like that."

"No." Bruno shook his head. "It won't work. Besides, I like my thoughts."

"Naturally."

He was tired. Maybe he should try to sleep for a while. His arms at his sides felt useless—what did he need them for?

I'm a man in recovery, he thought. I do need to rest. To heal. In fact, he was already on his way to recovery.

He turned and got a good look at her. His exclusive guardian angel. "I think I was dreaming before, some minutes ago. I was swimming in a very beautiful sea, maybe in Mexico. I was very happy in Mexico, but while I was swimming, I saw a man at my side reaching down with one hand and lifting a woman from the depths. I think she was blond, she seemed stiff, frozen-like. One of her arms was cut off at the elbow. And then, most strangely, the man dropped her and let her sink again, which made me think it must have been a plastic doll, not a real person, otherwise he wouldn't have done such a thing, letting her sink."

"What a frightful nightmare, Bruno."

"Yes, you see it as I describe it. A nightmare." He began to shake, and it took an effort to hold on to the bed. He felt sullied, unclean. Was he, in true fact, a sullied human being, or was it his contact with a certain kind of people that made him feel like someone who wasn't him at all? Maybe both. No one was innocent.

"Listen, Suzie, this is very important. Just now I understood we're all penitents. Our condition is one of penitence: the deeper the roots, the stronger the woods."

Suzie laughed. "Until I forget it, this should be easy to remember."

In a flash, he recalled the first movie he'd ever seen, oh, so long ago, *Seven Brides for Seven Brothers*. For some reason, Rose and Alexie had not joined them. It was just him and his father. For weeks afterward, his father hummed the song he liked best, the song the brothers sing in the snow as they chop wood. Bruno also loved the song, and when his father hummed it, Bruno hummed it, too, but mutely, because during such moments his father was elsewhere, calm and at peace.

Seeing now the anxious boy he had been, Bruno's throat tightened against the pebble of pain lodged there. The pain of the father transmitted to the child, the child ever eager to know more about his father's past, and yet, to spare the father the grief of buried memories, he never asked any questions, unless his father broached the subject first.

"I was a good child," he said. "I was obedient and respectful of my parents and the adults around me. And look at me now."

"I'm looking at you now," Suzie said, "and I can actually see it, see you, the cute small child trying to please everyone."

"You see it?" he asked, amazed.

"Yes, I do."

He shook his head. "Well, then. But how did I become the person I am now? Guarded, disillusioned, and often mistrustful of people's motives?"

"Well, Bruno, it's because you understand that all relationships are based on self-interest. And you, being the intelligent and uncompromising man that you are, see it as it is. You want to love and trust people, but you know you shouldn't, you'd be eaten alive. So you suffer. Still, try not to feel too bad about it. Like you said, we're all sufferers and penitents."

Indeed! How perfectly they saw eye to eye.

"Are you for real?" He giggled, a bit embarrassed. "What a silly question, but you know how it is, how strange it is when a dream comes true. And I had to come all this way to find you, my wonderful double, my reflection."

"This sounds like a love song."

"Well, yes," he admitted bashfully. "That's why I need to know you are real."

"I'm real, Bruno, quite real. We just happen to think alike."

"Amazing," he murmured. "What if my luck runs out? I feel so tired in my brain."

"Why don't you try to rest?"

"Rest?"

"Yes, why don't you?"

"Well, yes, I think I will." He wriggled his toes and realized he had no shoes on. "My shoes," he said.

"Don't worry about your shoes."

He shut his eyes, giving himself over to the soft cushions. How good it felt! "This is the most comfortable bed," he said. "I can feel my bones melting."

Somewhere in the room, Suzie laughed. He wondered if she was tired, if she wanted to lie down too, but frankly, he didn't feel like sharing the bed with her or anyone else. He wanted it all to himself. It was time he indulged his whims.

"What about you?" he felt obliged to ask. After all, he was only a guest.

"Don't worry about me, Bruno, I'm fine."

"Okay." He was the obedient child again. If only mommy came over and laid her hand on his forehead...

He slept. When he opened his eyes, it was still night or early dawn, or it was night again—he couldn't be sure, not that it mattered much. He was content, nothing bothered him, not physically, not mentally. This is not normal for me, he thought, but he let it go. What was normal, anyway? Things changed from day to day, from moment to moment.

"Well," he said with a smile, "you're not normal." As he spoke, he realized that even though he was talking to himself, Suzie might think he was talking about her, about her handicap, which, in fact, he had totally forgotten about. "I mean, you're not like everybody else, you're different from all the people I know."

"Well, thanks. I assume it's a compliment?"

Yes, he thought. He had run out of words, but this, too, was all right. He didn't have to talk if he didn't want to. Love offset everything. All at once, he wanted to laugh out loud straight from the heart. He felt empty, as though some giant hand had grabbed him by the ankle and shaken out all the agonies he had ever suffered. A newborn, he was open and receptive to whatever came his way.

"Are you all right?" he heard someone say, and he opened his eyes. Suzie's face was near his, so near he could smell her. He blinked several times to clear his vision. "Are you all right?" she asked, and he nodded. Of course he was all right. What else could he be?

"You're nagging me," he said genially. "No hard feelings, though. I do appreciate your concern. Someone once told me nothing is worth anything until you sell it, and then it's worth whatever you sold it for. Am I for sale?" he asked with sudden inspiration, and Suzie laughed.

Encouraged, he continued. "Do you remember Vaucanson's mechanical duck? It could flap its wings, it ate and defecated, and it was worth millions in French pride. The glory of France, Voltaire famously said. Imagine, Voltaire! I'm not boring you, I hope. I'm not a brilliant conversationalist."

"You sound brilliant to me, Bruno."

A feeling of wellbeing washed over him like a purifying stream. "Thank you, Suzie. You're the real thing, a real *mensch*! Mary and Ellen were too negative, maybe bitter. Something was always missing. When Mary couldn't find what she was looking for, she instantly accused someone, like the superintendent—he had keys to the apartment—or the maid. Everyone was a potential thief. Naturally, a few minutes later, she'd find what she was looking for, and then a sheepish yet triumphant smile would come to her lips, and she would look at me with shiny eyes, daring me to spoil her newly found joy. I don't know how such people can live in peace with themselves."

"Maybe they don't," Suzie said.

"Yes, maybe they don't." He turned pensive. "With Ellen, though, it was different. I mean, I don't blame her alone. I blame myself, too. Our marriage was tired, our sex was tired and, needless to mention, infrequent. We were both tired but afraid to admit it. And yet we did experience moments when a sudden spark would revive us both, a shared memory, a witty or funny remark, a burst of affection. And so, rather than stir things up and ask difficult questions, it was easier to look at the other as a necessary companion, like a useful item that's a bit old and rusty but still familiar and even comforting in certain ways."

Rose sighed. "That's how life runs its course, my son. It's unfortunate that our nature inclines us to remember the hurt we suffered from a friend or a spouse, but not the good that person has done us."

"Yes, you're right. And very wise! Thank you Suzie, you're a blessing."

"It's Rose, my son, not Suzie."

"Oh. How did you get here, Rose?"

"I haven't seen you in a while, so I figured…"

"I'm sorry I'm not myself at the moment. Maybe later we could have some coffee? Breakfast?"

"Yes, I'll look forward to it."

"Is Suzie still here?"

"Yes, Bruno, I'm here."

"Good, it's good to have you both nearby."

The funereal females at his fire. Ha! It all seemed so familiar and yet so remote, like a celestial *déjà-vu*.

Pas mal, eh, Rose?

Pas mal du tout, mon fils.

He slept and dreamt. It felt good to sleep and dream, toss from side to side, seek the cool side of the pillow. The sheets felt soft against his skin, so he was probably naked. Someone who cared had taken off his clothes and hung them somewhere. Probably Suzie. Good old and new Suzie. For them to have found each other as they did was nothing short of a miracle. Later, he would tell her that. Right now, like she said, he needed his rest. What had she put in his drink? The elixir of real life, something whispered in his brain, and he accepted it with a forgiving smile. All right, let it be, the elixir of real life, whatever it meant, whatever the consequences. He'll have plenty of time to worry about the consequences when he wakes from this ghostly episode.

"We spend our lives in limbo, don't we, Suzie? We have to accept it, we're all sleepwalkers."

"Even though I walk through the valley of the shadow of death, I will fear no evil, for you are with me."

"True, Suzie, how true!"

"I will never abandon you, Bruno."

Hot tears streamed down his face. "I know that, Suzie. I didn't trust you before, but I do now. I want people to know how I feel, even if too often people don't want to know how you feel. Rose and I went to see Molly when she was first transferred to an institution. She was heavily sedated and seemed very peaceful, as in a deep sleep. Once in a while, she licked her lips, and Rose said that ever since childhood, Molly had had this sexy way of licking her lips. It was a nervous tic, but it was still sexy, even now in her decrepit state.

"Molly had beautiful lips, full and sad, and this licking brought Molly back to Rose, for she knew that Molly, beyond the mania of her illness, was still there, even if only in her reflexes. It was sad to remember that many men had kissed those lips, although Molly never married. I went home afterward and for some crazy reason looked up the definition of French kissing in the dictionary. It said: *A passionate kiss with the lips parted and the tongues touching.* I cried and laughed when I read that.

"I need to tell Rose I fell in love with Molly when I was a baby. She had come to visit us and they tiptoed to my crib, and when I looked up, I saw this beautiful stranger in the dark bending over my crib and smiling at me with so much warmth and love, I distinctly remember that I smiled back, completely taken by her smiling face. Freud was right. We are sexual from day one. I'm even sure my small circumcised penis stood up to welcome her."

Bruno tried to rise, suddenly remembering he had to talk to Rose. "I have things to do," he said, but Suzie's strong arms held him back.

"You have to learn to relax, Bruno. If you rush through life, life rushes past you."

"Yes, but I have to speak to Rose…"

"Don't worry, Bruno, she knows."

"She knows?"

"Yes, she knows. Trust me, yes is better than no."

"All right, if you insist."

He heard footsteps. "Who goes there?" he called, feeling the terror of a blind man.

"It's me, Bruno, Celia."

"Ah, Celia, what a relief. You know I like you, Celia."

"I like you, too, Bruno."

"Celia, why is it so dark in here?"

"Because it's nighttime."

"Night? I thought rather early morning."

"No, Bruno, it's still night out."

"Morning comes after night, doesn't it?"

"Usually, yes." Celia laughed. She had a charming laugh, and Bruno wondered how many men had been seduced by her laugh. A charming Lilith!

"How did you and Mary meet?" Lilith asked.

"Oh, you've heard about Mary. Who told you? Rose?"

"No, Suzie."

"Where is she?"

"She had to go out for a moment, she'll be back soon. She asked me to come in and say hello."

"Hello, hello and welcome!" He felt giddy with joy. So much was happening in his quiet life, quiet no longer! "I'm very pleased you've made the trip to come and see me."

"I'm very pleased, too. So tell me, how did you and Mary meet?"

"Hmmm… How did we meet… Let me see. We met on a bus, actually, on the Hampton jitney, to be precise. I was going to meet up with friends for the weekend. It was a beautiful June day, and suddenly this woman gets on the bus and sits down right next to me. For years I've envied friends who were always lucky to find themselves sitting next to an exciting and attractive stranger during a flight or a bus ride. They always ran into someone on the street, someone they had wanted to run into, whereas I never did. The people I usually found myself sitting next to were dull, or worse, a mother with a cranky child. Never a woman I might fancy. And here I was, on the jitney, and this attractive blond chooses to sit next to me when there were other seats available. My lucky break, I thought, and for a while it was true."

"*C'est la vie*, as we say on the Continent."

"*Ah oui*." He laughed. "*La vie. La vida. La dolce vita.*"

"You're quite the language master."

"No, just a few vital words. Like, *la mort, la muerte*! Who would have thunk? There are so many women in my life at the moment. I feel very comfortable here with you and Suzie and all the others."

"Yes, but Suzie said you must rest."

Rest? He didn't want to rest. He was not an invalid, but who cares? Arguing led him nowhere.

"Well, I'm a good boy. I'm resting, but to tell you the truth, it tires me. How much longer must I rest? Life is not about rest."

"I don't know, Suzie is the chief nurse."

"You're funny, Celia. The chief nurse. She's your boss, isn't she? I don't think she'd appreciate this description of her."

"What do you mean?"

He tried to think. "Frankly, I'm not sure. It's the principle of the matter."

"Yes?"

He shook his head. "You must forgive me, I lost it. It's just that Mary used to say it a lot: I don't care about being right, it's the principle of the matter."

"That's okay, you mustn't tire yourself."

"No, I mustn't. Chief Nurse will be mad! "

Near his ear, Celia giggled. "You're a naughty little boy, Bruno. Do you want me to spank you a little?"

He giggled back at her. "I don't think that would be necessary."

"All right, then, do you want to tell me a story?"

"What kind of a story would you like to hear?"

"Whatever you want to tell me. I find you endearing and *very* amusing."

"Thank you, Celia, you have no idea how much your words please me." He thought a moment. "A story. I must have millions of them, but right this minute…" He continued to send searching beams into his brain, wanting to find a good story for Celia.

"Here's something, not a story exactly, but an important fact about me, your little Bruno. The only truth for me is poetic truth. The older I get, the more stupid and ignorant I feel, but still very thirsty for words, for wisdoms I can only find in books. Like Novalis said, *If the spirit sanctifies it, then every true book is a bible.*"

"Lovely," said Celia.

Ha! Bruno heard the echo of his voice. Indeed, his brain was on fire.

"What's so amusing? Please tell me," Celia said.

"I can't," he said slowly. "Why don't you tell me a story? Tell me what you thought when I walked into the place and ordered a whisky. You looked at me kind of condescendingly, letting me understand I didn't belong."

"Did I? I don't remember that. But I do remember I liked you as soon as you bummed a cigarette. I thought: Here's a man who knows what he wants and is not afraid to ask for it."

"Really? That's not how I see myself, but who knows? I usually feel I don't voice my wants at all or don't voice them enough. I always let others be loud, and more demanding. Demanding of me."

"Why do you allow it?"

"I'm not sure. Rose, my mother, is like that, too. Maybe I got it from her."

"Like a disease?"

"No!" He felt his face darken. "Please don't use such words, they're harmful."

"All right. I'm sorry if I hurt you."

He thought for a moment. "No, you didn't hurt me. Let's just forget it and go elsewhere."

"Where do you want to go?"

"I'm not sure yet. I have to think."

"All right, I'll wait."

Let her wait. Celia, his appointed Lilith!

"Are you wearing socks?" He suddenly remembered.

"Socks?" Celia laughed. "Why socks? Are you cold?"

"Never mind. Where's Suzie?"

"She's coming. Just a little while longer."

"I guess she has other clients? I'm not her only one."

"Clients? No, no clients, just friends."

"It's normal to be jealous, right? It's a normal feeling. I want to have normal feelings."

"It's very normal, but you needn't be jealous. She likes you very very much."

He smiled, pleased. "Thank you, Celia, you're a good person. You look tough, but you're good inside. I'll never go back to New York, to my old job. I'm in academia, you know, and I'm tired of all my colleagues. They're nice enough on a superficial level, but they're hard to take. I guess I'm hard to take, too. Life isn't easy for any of us. I forget who said it but it goes: *Poor heart, thy craving is for life, for love, for illusions!*

"At any rate, I wanted to feel I could depend on them, but I soon found out they held lofty ideals when it came to vague concepts such as freedom, love, and peace, but when it came to their petty personal affairs, when it came down to real, flesh-and-blood individuals, to face-to-face interactions, they turned ruthless, ferociously guarding what they considered their undisputed turf. They're vicious dogs. Worse. They wouldn't hesitate to stab you in the back if they deemed it a good career move."

"That's a shame."

"Shame indeed. I've been observing them for thirty some years, I know them. There are a few exceptions, of course, but they burn out sooner, justified in feeling they've been stepped on."

"Have you been stepped on?"

"Of course." Bruno laughed, feeling ecstatic. "That's why I'm getting out, enough is enough. Where's my Suzie?"

"I'm here, Bruno. You've been sleeping well, I gather?"

"No, I've been talking to Celia."

"Oh, good, I want the two of you to get to know one another."

"Why?"

"Why not? No need to be suspicious, you're not in New York."

"That's true, how silly of me! Why did you leave me? Where did you go?"

"Nowhere, Bruno, I'm right here."

"It's very confusing, but also cozy, this business. You all come and go like in the song."

"What song?"

"That song." He was alert enough to know he was confusing things, but he tried to remember anyway. "I forget now, maybe it'll come to me later. Are you wearing your sandal?"

"Yes, I'm wearing my sandal."

"No sock?"

"No, no sock. Why?"

"Because." He covered his mouth, howling into the blanket. "They say that demons have birds' feet and they wear socks to hide them when posing as humans. Lilith, my Lilith, was the first demon, I think. Feminists say she was the first feminist, disobeying God and Adam. She demanded better sex from Adam, and finally, when she realized she was not going to get what she wanted—women rarely do, as you know—she uttered the forbidden name of God, grew wings, and flew away from the Garden of Eden. She hid in a cave, where she had good sex with demons and bore them children. I feel so good," he said and stretched his limbs, sighing contentedly. "This is a good bed, my Suzie. Is it still night?"

"Yes, Bruno, it is."

"Nights here are long," he mused.

"Yes, they are, long and mild. May I quote you a line of poetry before you fall asleep?"

"Sure, please do."

"Whoever has seen beauty / Is already delivered over to death."

"It's beautiful, Suzie." He could feel his eyes burning with renewed faith. "Did you write it?"

"No, I came across it in a book."

All at once, he was filled with longing, the unending cycle of need—where will he go from here?

"Oh, Suzie, I'm suffering. I feel this pain, this apprehension. I'm scared. I want it to go away and leave me in peace."

"You're fine, Bruno, please don't shout."

"All right, all right." He tried to turn on his side, away from her, but couldn't. "I long for my father, Suzie. I'm beside myself with worry. I don't know where to turn. To whom."

Outside the window, a cluster of white fluffy clouds drifted past, and he looked for and found a man's hard face embedded in a cloud—his father. This was how the dead revealed themselves to the living, he thought, then realized the face did not really resemble his father's. Still, as he watched it, it turned into a reclining figure lying with its face down, and he thought it might be him, himself, on the bed. The sky was of the most delicate powder blue, and the soft, fluffy clouds were brilliantly white, like the cleanest, brightest bedsheets, so comforting and soothing.

"The horizon seems so much greater from here." An ugly cough escaped his throat—all the cigarettes he had smoked!

"Suzie, are you still here?"

"Yes, of course, dear Bruno."

"I missed his funeral, you know. I was away when he died."

"It wasn't your fault, it couldn't be helped."

"No, it couldn't. But his grave, I need to go to his grave. I haven't gone in so long, I'm ashamed. I have to attend to his stone."

"You'll go soon, Bruno, you have plenty of time."

Plenty of time, yes!

"I needed to tell you something important, and now I remember it very clearly. Can I hold your hand? Please?"

"I'm here, Bruno, tell me."

"It's not easy for me to admit, but as time passes, instead of becoming immune to hurt and pain, I'm becoming softer, more susceptible. I waver too much. Every little thing upsets me, even though I know I shouldn't let it. It's gotten to the point where I have to choose very carefully the people I see, because if someone aggravates me, he or she comes back at night to haunt me in my dreams." Suddenly, her image became vivid in his mind. "I see you in a different light."

"Really? What kind of different light?"

He needed to concentrate. He was talking gibberish, and Suzie tolerated him as one would tolerate a child or a drunk, but he had to impress on her that his thoughts were lucid, and that only when the words left his mouth they turned into something else. He wanted to tell her he felt his brain branching out, making connections he'd never made before. Indeed, he was beginning life all over again.

"There's too much noise in the world, Suzie, but I'm sure you know this already. Listen. We know our thoughts, but do we know why and how a thought or an image formed in our mind to haunt us? Can we even stop it? A shrink may try to explain it this way or that, but in the end it's all guesswork. The human heart, Suzie, how do we expect to cure it?"

He shut his eyes and saw the four letters of the forbidden Name of God, a name that had terrified him as a child. He imagined the wind, or the spirit of God, breathing in and out through the open vowels יהוה

How profound the mystery, the infinite depths of space in the open vowels! It was clear in his mind, yes, but was he allowed to utter it now? It was the Divine Name, his father had said, and one was not allowed to speak it. The various combinations of the letters held unimaginable power, and the Torah itself was in fact the Divine Name. If one letter was added or omitted, our world, God forbid, could be destroyed.

"Do not put me in a coffin, Suzie. You are my *shomer*, my beloved and loyal guard, so listen carefully and do not go hiding in a cave. Upon the death of a Jew, the eyes must be shut. You must cover the body, lay it on the ground, and light candles next to it. As a sign of respect, the body is not to be left alone, and is to be buried in a simple linen shroud, so that the poor and the rich receive the same honor. You may wrap my body in a *tallit*, if you find one around here."

Bruno chuckled. He should have told Suzie to cover the corpse, but he wasn't ready yet to see himself as a corpse. Still, like everything in life, it was better to be prepared. As with any undertaking, it was wise to take the first step rather than attempt to fathom the enormity of the task ahead and get discouraged. He heard music from afar and, to his surprise, tears of gratitude filled his eyes. He wanted to open his heart to all that was out there and become part of Creation. "I am asleep but my heart is awake," said the wisest of all men.

How small we are, small and diminishing. He saw himself in *shul* during the Kol Nidrei service, wrapped in a *tallit* and holding the prayer book close to *luach libbo*, the plate of his heart, when, miraculously, he noticed in the distance the Hasid mother kneeling at the foot of the stroller. She took a bite of the banana she held in her hand and chewed it into a mush, then fed it to her infant, mouth to mouth, like a bird feeding its young. He watched with fascination the baby's face, the purity of its expression, as it went for the mush in the mother's mouth.

Yes, Bruno thought. To be fed like this again, mouth to mouth, directly from the source, directly from the eternal calm.

About the Author

Novelist, and a translator of Hebrew literature, Tsipi Keller is the author of seventeen books, and the recipient of several literary awards, including National Endowment for the Arts Translation Fellowships, New York Foundation for the Arts Fiction Grants, and an Armand G. Erpf Translation Award from Columbia University. Individual translations have appeared in literary journals and anthologies in the U.S. and Europe, as well as in *The Posen Library of Jewish Culture and Civilization* (Yale University Press, 2012, 2020). Her most recent translations include Mordechai Geldman's *Years I Walked at Your Side* (SUNY Press, 2018); David Avidan's *Futureman* (Phoneme Media, 2017), and Erez Bitton's *You Who Cross My Path* (BOA Editions, 2015). Her latest novel, *Waves & Tonics,* was published by Ravenna Press in 2022.

BOOKS BY ITNA

Urban Gothic: The Complete Stories
Bruce Benderson

Crashing Cathedrals: Edmund White by the Book
Tom Cardamone

Tiny Fish that Only Want to Kiss
Gary Indiana

Everything Must Go
Lauren John Joseph

The Virtuous Ones
Christopher Stoddard